SEEKING JUSTICE

A CHRISTIAN ROMANTIC SUSPENSE

FINNEGAN FIRST RESPONDERS

LAURA SCOTT

Copyright © 2022 by Laura Iding

All rights reserved.

No part of this book may be reproduced in any form or by any electronic or mechanical means, including information storage and retrieval systems, without written permission from the author, except for the use of brief quotations in a book review.

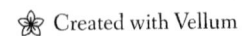

❀ Created with Vellum

CHAPTER ONE

Huddled in her knee-length, down-filled winter coat, Joy Munson stamped her feet to ward off the numbness as she waited outside Paulie's Pub for Detective Tarin Finnegan. She'd learned Paulie's was a cop hangout and had come several nights in a row after work to see if Tarin showed. Tonight, he'd come in with another guy, maybe his partner. She'd noticed Tarin didn't drink anything but club soda, and when he'd finished, she'd quickly headed outside, expecting him to leave shortly thereafter.

Fifteen minutes later, she was still waiting. She hadn't wanted to confront the detective in front of his partner or any of the other officers inside, but she wasn't sure how much longer she'd be able to hang around in the icy February wind either. She stayed close to the wall to avoid the worst of the wind. When her teeth started to chatter, she jumped up and down in a vain attempt to warm up.

Just as she was about to go back inside, she noticed Tarin heading for the door—his red hair made it easier to spot him. Now that the moment was upon her, she was nervous about approaching him.

He stepped outside and turned toward her.

"Detective Finnegan?" She stepped forward, pasting a smile on her face. "I don't know if you remember me . . ."

"Joy Munson." He gave her a brief nod. "I remember. How are you?"

Oddly, she was surprised he'd remembered her since she hadn't seen him in five years. "I need a moment of your time, may I walk with you?"

He eyed her warily but shrugged. "You can walk where you want, but I'm not sure I can help you."

You're the only one who can, she thought wearily.

She fell into step beside him. The small parking lot was down and around the corner, so she didn't have much time. "I need detailed information on my brother's case."

"Why?" Tarin asked bluntly. "His death was ruled a suicide."

"I told you five years ago, Ken didn't kill himself!" She didn't bother to hide her anger. "He would never do that. And he certainly didn't take drugs. As far as the suicide note, it was either faked or he was forced to write it."

Tarin didn't say anything as he continued walking.

Gritting her teeth, she tried again. "Listen, I recently learned something new. The doctor who'd prescribed those narcotics Ken supposedly overdosed on was arrested for overprescribing pain pills. And get this, once they looked into his practices, the authorities found several million dollars hidden in offshore accounts. Ken was a pharmacy resident at the time, less than a year from becoming a full-fledged pharmacist, and I think he stumbled upon the ruse that was being done by the doc and maybe even the pharmacist Ken was working for." She stopped and put a hand on Tarin's arm, stopping his progress and forcing him to face her. "My brother was murdered, and I intend to prove it."

"Ms. Munson, I can't share police information with you." He sounded annoyed now, which hadn't been her intent. "I appreciate how you feel, but it's best if you leave the police work to me. I'll be in touch if I learn anything new."

She blew out a frustrated breath, sensing she wouldn't get anything more from Detective Finnegan. "Fine. But please, call me Joy." She turned away so quickly her foot slipped on the icy sidewalk. She lost her balance, flailing her arms to catch herself before she hit the ground.

At the exact same time, a gunshot echoed through the night.

"Get down!" Tarin pulled his weapon and rushed over to pull her toward the closest building. Then he stood in front of her, covering her with his body.

At first, she was confused until she realized he believed the gunfire was intended for her specifically rather than a random event. But that was impossible. She hadn't told anyone about her intent to pursue an investigation into her brother's death.

Besides, Dr. Eli Lewis was in jail. Who would bother to come after her now?

The crime rate in the city of Milwaukee had been growing worse each year. Not as bad as Chicago but gunfire was not an unusual occurrence. She was certain the gunfire was related to something else, not her.

"This is Detective Finnegan reporting gunfire at the corner of Bayside Street and Calvin. Requesting backup!"

"What's going on?" She tried to peek around him, but he used one arm to tuck her behind his back.

"Don't move." She knew from her interaction with him after her brother's death that Detective Finnegan was a man of few words. His head turned from side to side as he

His gaze clung to hers, and despite the darkness, she could see she'd caught his attention. "The doc was arrested?"

"Yes. You can search on Dr. Eli Lewis for yourself. Apparently, he'd gone on the run but was found in Mexico after six months of hiding from the feds."

Tarin stared at her for a long moment. "New evidence might be enough to reopen the case, although it won't be easy. Five years have passed, which means the case is colder than ice. And there's also the fact that the medical examiner already ruled your brother's death a suicide. The doctor's arrest alone isn't enough. We'd need proof that your brother uncovered something incriminating against Lewis as a motive for murder."

And that was exactly why she was here tonight. "Detective Finnegan, please, I really need your help." She tried not to show the extent of her desperation. "I know you may not be able to officially reopen Ken's case, but I would still like to see the original police reports, the interviews, et cetera. Maybe looking at things with a new eye and knowing Lewis has been arrested will help us find that connection."

"Us?" He frowned. "If I remember correctly, you're an accountant not a cop."

Again, she was surprised he'd remembered that much about her. "True, but being an accountant has taught me to be meticulous about details." A trait that had come in handy in her role of doing internal audits. "If I can just look at the information..."

"I'll look at it, but I won't make any promises. I seriously doubt anything will come of it." He turned away, but she wasn't letting him go that easily.

"Detective, I want to be involved." She quickly caught up to him. "Can't you understand? I need to do something scanned the area. "Who knows you came to ask me about your brother's death?"

"No one. I didn't say a word to anyone about reopening my brother's case."

Wailing sirens reverberated through the night, and she relaxed knowing help was on the way. Tarin didn't budge, though, until two squads, their red and blue lights flashing, pulled up in front of them.

"Finnegan? Is that you?" one of the officers called. "Anyone hurt?"

"We're fine. I'm here with a civilian, Joy Munson." He finally stepped forward to meet up with the officers. "I believe the gunfire came from the north. I'd like at least two officers to head that way to search for evidence."

Deciding it was best to stay close, she joined the officers.

"Will do." Three of the four turned away and split up to do the search. One officer stayed behind, eyeing her curiously before turning to Tarin. "What happened?"

"Someone took a shot at Ms. Munson. Thankfully, she wasn't hit, maybe because she slipped on the ice." He turned to scan behind them. "Unfortunately, the slug could be anywhere. I didn't hear it hit anything."

"We'll take a look," the officer said. "Ms. Munson, any idea why you might be a target?"

"None." She wondered if she should mention her brother's death, but then another thought occurred to her. "I am working on an internal audit of a large bank. It's a big project, and I've already found some irregularities. Just yesterday my boss advised me to dig deeper."

Tarin turned to look at her in surprise. "Which bank?"

She hesitated. "I'm not really supposed to talk about it."

"This is a police investigation," Tarin said with a frown. "You need to tell us who has a motive to kill you."

"Kill me?" She paled. "There's no reason for someone to do something so drastic over an audit. If I was gone, they'd just hire another accountant to take over." When Tarin continued to stare at her, she sighed, and added, "Okay, fine. Trustworthy Bank. But if you want any more information, I'll need to call my boss." It wasn't lost on her that she'd asked Tarin to provide information to her about her brother's death when she couldn't return the favor now. It was a difficult situation to be in the middle of.

Easy to understand his reticence.

The officer scribbled the information into a notebook. She wondered if Tarin would mention her brother's death, but he didn't.

Because he didn't believe the information to be relevant? She hadn't been lying about not saying anything to anyone about her intent to dig into her brother's death.

She shivered. Hopefully, the evidence would prove the gunfire was related to something else entirely.

Because it was difficult to believe her boring life as an accountant had catapulted her into danger.

AFTER A QUICK INTERNAL debate over whether he should confide in the officer about the reason Joy Munson had sought him out, Tarin had decided against it. Even if Joy had mentioned her intent to dig into her brother's death to a friend, it wasn't likely that information would result in gunfire this fast.

Especially since the investigation had been closed for five years. Joy's talking to him didn't mean anything. Asking for help was hardly a threat.

No, the more he thought about it, the more he leaned

toward her job as an internal auditor as the reason she was targeted. He wanted to know exactly what sort of irregularities she'd uncovered. Something serious enough to kill for? Granted, she'd made a good point about someone else being assigned to the case if she was injured or worse, dead, but for all he knew, the shot was nothing more than a warning.

One he intended to take very seriously. Not that this was his case. In fact, quite the opposite. Since he'd been on scene and involved as a witness, he knew full well the case would be handed over to another detective.

The thought made him scowl. Being here when the incident happened had made it personal. He wanted to see it through.

Joy was shivering in the cold, so he gestured for Officer Nelson to come over. "Would you mind allowing Ms. Munson to wait in the squad?"

"Of course. This way, Ms. Munson." Nelson gestured toward the vehicle.

"I—I'd r-rather stay h-here." Her teeth were chattering now too.

He swallowed a sigh. "You're freezing. Do you have a car here? I can escort you to your vehicle if you'd prefer. We'll let you know if we find anything."

She shook her head but jogged in place to warm up. "I—walked from work. My c-car is in the sh-op, so I've been riding the b-bus."

Tarin didn't like the idea of Joy riding the bus at night, especially after being used as target practice. As much as he wanted to stick around, he knew the officers didn't need his help. He glanced at Nelson, who shrugged. "We're good if you want to head home."

Leaving went against his instincts, but watching Joy shiver bothered him. As the second oldest of nine kids, he couldn't stand to see her suffer. If his sister was there, he'd insist on taking her home. "Okay, let's go, then. I'll drive you home."

She hesitated as if sensing he didn't want to leave, then nodded. "Th-thank you."

"It's not a problem." He took her arm and steered her down the sidewalk and around the corner to the small lot where he'd parked his SUV. The hour wasn't late, only seven o'clock in the evening, but he was hungry. And based on the way Joy, er, Ms. Munson had mentioned not having a car, he figured she hadn't eaten anything either.

And why he was concerned with her welfare, he had no idea. She was an accountant for Pete's sake; they must pay her well. *Probably better than I earn as a detective*, he thought. No one went to work in the police force looking for big bucks. It was a calling, a dedication to protecting and serving the public. To be a first responder, running toward danger rather than away.

His parents had been amazing role models. Losing them ten years ago, when he had only been twenty-five, had been incredibly difficult. His older brother Rhyland had instantly moved back home to step in as head of the family. Tarin hadn't hesitated to help his brother keep their siblings together, although he hadn't been thrilled with the need to move back to the Finnegan homestead.

Tarin's second brush with death had been when he'd lost his partner, Caroline. He and Caroline had just started seeing each other on a personal level, although they'd been partners for a full year by then. He hadn't even introduced her to the family, partially because he knew Rhyland would make a big deal out of Tarin dating his partner. And now he understood why.

He and Caroline had responded to a scene that was

supposed to have been cleared, but more gunfire had erupted, hitting and killing Caroline on the spot. He remembered screaming until he was hoarse about an officer being down, but even as he scrambled toward her, he'd known it was too late to save her.

He wondered now if losing Caroline so close to being assigned Ken Munson's case had hindered him more than he'd realized. Was it possible he'd missed some key piece of evidence that might have led him down the path of viewing the case as a homicide? Failure was a bitter pill to swallow, but it wouldn't be the first time.

He'd failed to keep Caroline safe that night five years ago. That fact only reinforced his need to keep Joy safe.

"Detective?" Joy's voice drew him from his troublesome thoughts. "Are you okay?"

"Yeah. Sorry about that." He realized he'd been standing near his SUV without moving. He pulled out his key fob and unlocked the car. He reached for the passenger door handle. "You may as well call me Tarin."

She nodded and slid into the passenger seat. "If you'll call me Joy."

"It's a deal, Joy." He closed her door and jogged around to get in behind the wheel. He turned on the car engine and gave it a few minutes to warm up. Soon, heat was blasting through the vents, and the seat warmers were activated. He told himself it was easier to be on a first-name basis; all this Detective and Ms. Munson stuff would get wearisome.

It didn't mean anything. Granted, Joy was beautiful, with her wavy blond hair framing her face and her bright hazel eyes, but she was off-limits.

The way Caroline had been.

This time, he silently vowed, he would not make the

mistake of becoming personally involved. He'd learned his lesson.

"Where do you live?" he asked as he drove through the parking lot.

"I have a condo in Brookland." She sighed and relaxed against the seat. "Thanks for the ride. I was cold."

"Yeah, your chattering teeth was a big clue." He was surprised she lived in the same Milwaukee suburb as the Finnegan homestead, but he didn't mention it. He didn't live there, he lived in Oakdale.

"Detec—er, Tarin, I hope the events tonight don't distract you from looking into my brother's case."

What? He turned to stare at her for a moment, before turning his attention to the road. "Don't you think being targeted by gunfire is more important than the possibility of reopening a cold case?"

Joy lifted her chin. "There's no evidence that I was targeted tonight on purpose. For all we know, there was some drug thing going on nearby. You're a detective, you know better than anyone that the crime rate has gotten worse over the past few years. Why do you think I moved to Brookland?"

"There's crime in Brookland too," he protested, although she was right about the worsening crime rate in Milwaukee. His and Dave's caseload was already overwhelming, without adding the additional time he'd need to investigate Ken Munson's death.

"I know, but it's not the same." She sighed, then added, "I know you must be super busy, but I was hoping you would still look into my brother's case."

"I said I would." He wasn't perfect, had made mistakes, but he was a man of his word. "But considering what transpired tonight, you may want to keep this conversation with me a secret."

"I will. As I mentioned earlier, I haven't told anyone my plans to ask you to look at Ken's case."

"Not even your closest friend?"

"No, Sarah and her husband, Luke, got married last year, and they bought a house, so she hasn't had time to get together." She honestly missed her best friend but completely understood that Sarah's husband had to come first.

"What about the guy you were dating, Kevin Creek?"

Her jaw dropped. "How did you remember that?"

He couldn't help but smile. "I don't know, weird details seem to stick in my brain."

"I bet that helps in your line of work," she said . "No, things with Kevin didn't work out."

He shouldn't have been glad to hear she wasn't with the guy, but at the time, he hadn't much cared for Kevin. He'd come across as rather arrogant; his attitude had rubbed Tarin the wrong way. Then again, a lot of people didn't think highly of the cops.

Unless, of course, they needed police protection.

Whatever. Joy's personal life, or lack thereof, wasn't any of his business. He decided to trust that she was being honest about not telling anyone of her plans to reopen her brother's case, which made him think her job of doing the internal audit may be the reason for the gunfire. Since he really wanted to get back down to the crime scene, he focused on taking the closest route to Brookland. "What's your address?"

She rattled it off, and he was surprised to realize her condo was only two miles from the Finnegan homestead.

"I grew up in that area." He didn't elaborate. "How long have you lived here?"

"Four years." She stared down at her hands for a moment. "Most of my brother's savings went to pay his student loans, but there was some left over for me. I didn't really want to take it but ended up using half for the down payment of the condo. I gave the other half to charity, one that provided funds for people seeking help from drug and alcohol addiction."

"That was incredibly generous." He couldn't help but admire her decision. He knew better than most that people would kill each other for far less.

"Not really. If I hadn't needed a new place to live, I would have donated more. The good news is that I've been able to donate more money to the charity every year now. Even though I know my brother didn't take those drugs voluntarily, I still think it's a worthy cause."

"I couldn't agree more. I've seen firsthand what drug and alcohol abuse does to families." In those cases where substance abuse wasn't a factor, greed and jealousy were the highest driving forces in all homicide cases. Thinking about it now, he realized the greed part may relate to Joy's brother's death, the way she so firmly believed.

It wasn't a stretch to think that her brother had stumbled onto the big scheme Dr. Eli Lewis had concocted, especially in Ken's role as a pharmacy resident in training. Tarin needed to understand more about how pain medications were reimbursed by insurance companies. If Lewis had been able to squirrel away a few million dollars, there had to be a way for him to get that money based on each prescription he provided.

He was about to ask if Joy knew anything about the

process when he realized her condo was just ahead. Closer to the Finnegan homestead than he'd thought.

He pulled into the driveway and reached for the button to shut down the engine.

"No need, you can just let me out here." Joy quickly reached for the door handle. "No reason to get out of the warm car."

"Hold on, Joy, you're not walking in alone." He shut off the engine. His mother was gone, but he knew she would shake her head in disappointment if he didn't escort her to the door. He slid out from behind the wheel, then hurried around to her side. "You should leave a light on, it's safer than coming home to a dark house."

"Is that what you do?" Joy asked with a cheeky smile.

"I'm a cop and carry a gun," he countered. "And yes, we make sure our sisters always leave a light on, no matter what."

"Sisters?" she echoed, stopping in front of the door to dig her key from her purse. "How many?"

"Three sisters and five brothers." He turned to scan the area. Joy's condo was in a wooded area of the subdivision, not unlike the house he grew up in. Then his gaze narrowed on a car coasting down the street without lights or sounds of a car engine. A Tesla maybe? The passenger window lowered, and when he saw the barrel of a gun, he reacted instinctively, pushing Joy out of harm's way and pulling his weapon. "Stop, police!"

For the second time in an hour, gunfire echoed throughout the night. Only this time, the bullets embedded themselves in the door of Joy's condo, inches from his head.

CHAPTER TWO

After dropping to the ground, Joy turned to see a dark vehicle sliding silently past, quickly disappearing from sight. Her heart thundered in her chest, fear coating her tongue. This was the second time someone had taken a shot at her! But why? The internal audit she was doing for Trustworthy Bank?

"Are you hurt?" Tarin asked.

"No." Frightened to death didn't count, so she pushed herself upright and stepped back onto the porch. "What about you?"

"Fine." His tone was curt, and she could tell he was not happy. "I need you to get back into my SUV."

Confused, she asked, "Shouldn't we call the Brookland police?"

"Already done. But I need you to get inside the SUV for now. When the police arrive, we'll check the house and decide what to do from there."

Decide what to do? Again, she wasn't sure she understood, but she allowed Tarin to steer her toward his car. When she was settled in the front passenger seat, he hurried around to drop the key fob on the seat, then started the engine.

"You don't have to waste your gas," she protested, but he didn't respond as sirens approached.

"Stay warm." He gave her a quick nod, then closed the door.

Shivering, she reached over to turn on the seat warmers. Her car didn't have them, and now that she'd experienced them for herself, she wondered how anyone made it through a Wisconsin winter without them.

Yet even as heat seeped through the leather seats, her shivering didn't stop. She was scared and still grappling with the knowledge that she'd been shot at twice in one night.

Her life was boring. This sort of thing didn't happen to women like her. Losing her parents and then her brother a few years later had been the biggest events of her life up until now.

She'd have thought this was all related to her brother's death if not for the fact that she truly hadn't told anyone her plan to ask Tarin Finnegan to reopen the case. Unless she'd been followed just in case she decided to do such a thing? No, that didn't make sense either. No one would follow her to the bank and home to her condo for days on end.

But there was no denying she was in danger. Glancing over, she could see that Tarin was pointing to several dark areas on her front door. It took a moment for her to realize they were bullet holes.

Bullet holes!

Now she understood what he'd meant by figuring out their next steps. Obviously staying here wasn't an option. Going to her friends Sarah and Luke's house wasn't an option; she refused to put them in danger.

She shivered again, a wave of helplessness hitting hard. She was on her own, at least until the police figured out who was behind these attacks.

Watching Tarin speaking to the Brookland police, it was obvious to her that he was in charge. Either because he held the rank of detective or because it was normal for him to be in control.

To be honest, she figured it was the latter. Even if Tarin had been a patrol officer, she had no doubt he'd act the same way. There was something—commanding—about him. Maybe because he had a large family. She'd been shocked to hear he had three sisters and five brothers. The bullets had started flying before she could find out more.

After what seemed like forever, but was only twenty minutes, Tarin and the Brookland officers came over to the car. Tarin opened her door. "Joy? Officer Banfield would like to talk to you."

"Ah, okay." She reached over to shut off Tarin's car, then slid out to face the officer. "I'm not sure I have much to contribute. I was about to unlock my door when Tar—er, Detective Finnegan pulled me out of harm's way. I heard the gunfire and saw a black car without any lights moving silently down the street."

"Did you hear the sound of a car engine?" Officer Banfield asked.

"No, and that was weird. It was as if it was a ghost car or something, not that I believe in such things," she hastened to add.

"It was either a Tesla or some other electric car," Tarin said. "As there were no taillights, I didn't get a plate number either. I returned fire but can't say for certain I hit the vehicle."

"We'll make a note to check all the garages in the area

for any electric vehicles coming in with bullet holes." Officer Banfield shrugged. "But you know as well as I do there are plenty of places to take a car where the owners wouldn't bother to make a report."

"I know." Tarin scowled. "This is the second attempt at Ms. Munson in the past hour. I need you to collaborate with MPD, sharing details of both events. We need to find this shooter, and soon."

"Understood. I'll let our lieutenant know." Officer Banfield seemed to take Tarin's concerns to heart. "I'll have him call you."

"Thanks, appreciate it." Tarin waved at the door. "We need those slugs sent to the crime lab too. None were found at the scene earlier, but it's still best to have them on file."

Joy paled, realizing what Tarin meant. That they needed the evidence in case the shooter tried again.

Her knees felt weak, so she leaned against the side of Tarin's SUV. This was so not her world, she was accustomed to spreadsheets and data.

Not prying bullets out of her front door.

"Will you give me your key? I'd like to go through the house." Tarin held out his palm, looking at her expectantly.

"Sure." She pulled the keys from her purse and dropped them into his hand. "But if I have to spend the night at a hotel, I'd like to pack a bag."

He frowned, then nodded. "Okay, give me a few minutes."

In reality, he took a full fifteen minutes before returning. "Nice place, I don't think anyone has been inside."

She shivered again, and not from the cold. Doing her best to remain composed, she headed inside to pack a bag. Tarin stood behind her like a sentinel on duty. And maybe he was. She appreciated having his protection over the past hour. If he hadn't been there, she'd likely be dead.

The sobering thought brought tears to her eyes. She subtly wiped them away before turning to face Tarin. Lifting the small suitcase off the bed, she faced him. "I'm ready."

"Good." He took the bag from her hand. Maybe he noticed the dampness around her eyes because his voice softened as he added, "Don't worry, I'll keep you safe."

A lump formed in the back of her throat, making it impossible to speak. She followed him through her house, then abruptly paused when she saw her laptop computer. Without hesitation, she unplugged it from the wall and scooped it up.

Tarin noticed her actions. "Do you have a laptop case?"

She found her voice. "In my room. Hold on a minute." She turned and hurried back for the case. After tucking the laptop and cord inside, she returned to the main living area. "I'm ready."

Ready for what? She wasn't quite sure. Tarin was his usual quiet self, so he didn't offer any information as he stored her suitcase and laptop in the rear of the vehicle. Then he opened her passenger door for her.

She couldn't remember the last time a man had done that for her, certainly not her ex-boyfriend, Kevin. Instead of offering her support and kindness, the guy had broken things off after her brother's death. Proving he hadn't really cared about her at all.

The breakup had hurt, especially as she'd also been grieving her brother's death, but she knew she was better off without him.

Tarin slid in behind the wheel, then slowly backed out of her driveway. She tried to think of the closest hotels, but her mind was a complete blank. "Uh, Tarin? Do you have a place in mind?"

"I do." He glanced at her. "There's a motel not far from here called the American Lodge, it's owned by a former firefighter." He paused, then added, "Or you can come to my place to stay in the guest room. No strings attached of course, I don't get personally involved with victims. Normally I wouldn't do this, but I think it's more important for you to feel safe. And I'm hungry. I was thinking I could throw together a couple of burgers if you'd like."

He was offering food and lodging while making it clear she shouldn't expect anything more. Accountants were known to be logical, and spending the night at his place was the complete opposite of that. Yet she also couldn't imagine sitting alone in a motel room. "I wouldn't mind going to your place if you're sure it's no trouble. I don't want to be a bother, I plan to head to work early in the morning anyway."

"Work?" He frowned again, making her realize she'd never once seen him smile. "Not a good idea."

She blinked, surprised by his comment. "I can't just take off. I have a job to do."

If anything, the scowl lines deepened. "We'll discuss your options later. I live in Oakdale, but I plan to take the side streets. It may take a little longer than normal."

"I thought you lived in Brookland?" She thought back, realizing he'd mentioned growing up there. No shock that he didn't live there any longer.

He hesitated, then shook his head. "No, but some of my family still do."

"You really have three sisters and five brothers?"

"Yeah." For the first time, he offered a wry smile. "I'm the second oldest of nine siblings."

"Wow." She thought about the relationship she'd shared with her brother. They'd been relatively close, more so after their parents had died, each within a few years of the other from different types of cancer. "I can't even imagine."

"Never a dull moment, that's for sure," Tarin said.

He kept a keen eye on the rearview mirror as they drove in the general direction of Oakdale, another Milwaukee suburb located slightly southwest of Brookland. Between Tarin's strong presence and the heated seats, she finally stopped shivering.

But when he pulled up to the driveway of his small house, her nerves began to flutter all over again. It wasn't that she didn't trust, Tarin, she did. She'd been the one to seek him out tonight.

Yet deep down, she knew the moment she walked into his personal space, her life would change forever.

IDIOT, he silently admonished. Tarin had been kicking himself the entire drive to his place. He never should have given Joy a choice as to where she wanted to go. He should have just driven her straight to the American Lodge.

Last month, he'd ripped into his older brother, Rhy, over his decision to bring Devon, a woman who was also in danger, to the Finnegan homestead. In his opinion, Rhy had taken a huge risk, considering their three youngest siblings still lived at home. Aiden and Alanna were twins, and the youngest, also known as the oops baby, Elly, was still in her EMT program, scheduled to graduate in May.

As he parked in the one-car garage and opened Joy's door, he was forced to admit this wasn't much different from what Rhy had done. Bringing a woman he barely knew into his private space was not smart.

Too late now. Swallowing a sigh, he pulled her suitcase and laptop from the back and carried them inside. He carried them straight to the guest room. "Here you go. I'll get dinner started."

"Would you like help?"

"No thanks." He forced a tight smile, then hightailed it out of there. He reminded himself that this was a temporary arrangement. Tomorrow, he'd get her set up in a hotel, maybe one close to the Trustworthy Bank.

He pulled the hamburger from his fridge and went to work, trying not to think of the very attractive woman making herself comfortable in his guest room. One night, then he'd come up with a new plan.

The idea of her going into work the following morning, though, concerned him. He was convinced she was in danger over whatever inconsistencies she'd uncovered while performing her audit. What she needed was a bodyguard, but he couldn't perform that role. He was scheduled to work the next several days, and they were short-staffed as it was. No way could he ask for time off to watch over her at the bank.

Maybe she could work from here via her laptop? Something to consider.

"Are you sure there isn't anything I can do to help?"

He glanced over his shoulder to see Joy hovering nearby. "No thanks, have a seat. This shouldn't take long. I hope you're not expecting anything too fancy."

"I hadn't realized how hungry I was until I smelled the burgers cooking," she admitted, dropping into the closest kitchen chair. "I owe you my life, Tarin. I very much appreciate everything you're doing for me."

"My job is all about protecting the public." Even as he said the words, he knew that wasn't the only reason he'd brought Joy here. No, he'd already formed some strange bond with her, one that had started five years ago when he'd gone to notify her in person about her brother's death.

Knowing the doc who had prescribed the meds her brother had supposedly taken was now in jail was very interesting. And if he were honest, he'd admit he wanted nothing more than to dig into the case further. Maybe not tonight, it was already getting late, but he made a note to find time to reopen the file tomorrow.

And for now, he'd keep his decision to review his five-year-old notes to himself, not bothering his partner, Dave, or his boss about his plan. No need to do that unless he ended up formally reopening the investigation.

A move his boss would not appreciate. His partner, Dave Crowley, wouldn't be thrilled either. He could already hear Dave complaining that they had enough open and ongoing investigations on their plates without adding a five-year-old closed case to the pile.

And he'd be right.

Tarin knew he may have to work on the case on his own time. He removed the burgers from the indoor grill and slid them onto large buns, setting them on a plate. After carrying them to the table, he added another plate of sliced tomatoes, lettuce, and cheese to the table along with condiments.

"Looks amazing," Joy said with a smile. "Thank you."

"I was hungry, remember?" He hadn't done anything special other than adding a burger or two for her. "I'll say grace, if you don't mind." Without waiting for her response, he bowed his head. "Dear Lord, we thank You for this food we are about to eat. We ask You to bless this food while continuing to keep us safe in Your loving care. Amen."

"Amen," Joy said softly. Then she looked at him curiously. "I didn't realize you prayed before meals."

"How could you?" He shrugged and handed her the plate of food first. "We were raised to pray before meals, and after our parents died, we kept up the tradition."

"I'm sorry for your loss," she murmured.

"We both have suffered losses." He'd lost Caroline, too, but he didn't mention that part.

"Yes, we have. Our—er, my parents died within two years of each other, both from different kinds of cancer." She grimaced as she added lettuce, tomato, and cheese to her burger along with liberal amounts of ketchup. "Ken and I remained close, but after losing him . . ." Her voice trailed off.

"I'm sure that was incredibly difficult." He vaguely remembered making a note about their parents passing away in his report. "My oldest brother, Rhyland, insisted we move back home after losing our parents to keep the family together. After a few years when there were only the twins and Elly left, I bought this place." He waved a hand at the house. "It's small, but I don't need a lot of room."

"It's nice and cozy." She took a bite of her burger and sighed. "So good," she said between chews.

For several moments, they enjoyed the meal. His brother, Rhy, was the fastest eater among the Finnegan siblings. Just to be different, Tarin made it a point to eat slowly, savoring the meal. However, he was hungry enough to make that more difficult than usual.

He'd made four burgers, eating two himself. "There's one more for you."

"No, thanks." Joy's smile slowly faded as she stared

down at her lap. "I'm a little surprised I was able to eat at all considering everything that happened."

"You're safe here," he told her. "I know we weren't followed from your place. And no one would think to look for you here."

"I know. Thanks again for bringing me here." She wiped her mouth, then stood. "In return, I'll pitch in by doing the dishes."

"You don't have to," he protested.

"Yes, it's the least I can do." She began filling the sink. "I truly don't mind."

He could understand where she was coming from, pitching in was something his siblings always would have insisted on doing as well. He gave her a quick nod. "Okay, thanks."

"Will you be involved in investigating the shooting incidents?" she asked.

After finishing his second burger, he stood and carried his plate and water glass to the sink. "I'm a witness, so the upper brass won't allow me to do that. But I plan to be kept in the loop on what they find."

"That's reassuring."

He was touched by her faith in him and hoped he wouldn't let her down. He was known as a bulldog with incredible persistence, but he was also up against the head honchos who would try just as hard not to include him in the information flow. He pulled out a dish towel and began drying dishes. "Is there any way you can work from here via your laptop?"

She pursed her lips for a moment. "I could maybe do that if the bank will allow me to have remote access. But it's easier, really, to be at the bank to do the work."

"Humor me," Tarin said. "It's best you don't go in

tomorrow. Get in touch with the bank officials first thing tomorrow morning to see if they'll allow you to work remotely. I have to go to the precinct, so I can't stay with you at the bank while you work."

"I didn't ask you to come with me," she said, giving him a pointed look. "These attacks happened at night, I'm sure it's safe enough during the day."

"I wouldn't call gunfire in early evening as safe enough," he shot back. "These guys may be more desperate than ever to take another shot at you."

She blanched. "You're just trying to scare me."

"I'm being honest." He wasn't going to gloss over the danger. "I can escort you to the bank, if necessary, but I can't stay the entire day."

She sighed and reluctantly nodded. "Okay, fine. I get it. I'll see what the bank manager says about allowing remote access. But if that's not an option, I'm still going to work. My job is important to me, Tarin. I can't just blow it off."

He ground his teeth together but didn't say anything more. It was hard to be angry with her dedication to her profession.

Yet her safety needed to be a top priority. Even if he could find some other cop to watch over her, it wasn't likely they'd do the job for free.

And for all he knew, the bank wouldn't allow a private bodyguard on the premises following her around anyway.

After finishing the dishes, Joy stepped away from the sink. "Thanks again, Tarin. I'm going to try to get some sleep."

"Good idea." He dried the last two plates, then tucked them in the cupboard. "Good night."

"Good night." Her smile didn't quite reach her eyes as she slipped past him.

He removed his laptop from the corner of the counter and quickly logged on. It didn't take him long to find the story about the manhunt and ultimate arrest of Dr. Eli Lewis. Scanning the article, his pulse kicked up at the information. The guy had allegedly written thousands of prescriptions, using a variety of pharmacies and different doctor names across the city, which had been eventually noticed by a new, sophisticated tracking system.

Interesting that he was able to use different doctor names. He knew that ordering narcotics required a DEA number, assigned by the Drug Enforcement Agency. Maybe Lewis had found retired doc names and numbers to steal.

One thing was for sure, Lewis had made several million off his scheme. No doubt in his mind that was the kind of cash worth killing over. And who better than a doc to make the death look like a suicide in a way good enough to fool the medical examiner.

With a yawn, he closed his computer. He'd find the time to dig into Ken Munson's death tomorrow. After he poked around to get information about the two attempts against Joy.

Tarin didn't expect to get much sleep, but when his alarm went off at six o'clock, he sat bolt upright, blinking in the darkness. His first thought was of Joy—he hadn't had a guest stay over that wasn't one of his siblings since he'd moved in. He showered and changed into his suit coat, tie, and dress slacks before emerging from the bedroom.

The door to the guest room was still closed. Relaxing a bit, he headed into the kitchen to start a pot of coffee. And nearly choked on his own spit when he saw Joy sitting at the table, working on her laptop.

"You're up?" He inwardly winced at the inane words.

"I had trouble sleeping. Not because of the room, it was very comfortable, but I couldn't shut down my mind." She tapped her temple. "Squirrel brain happens more often than I care to admit."

He nodded, having been kept awake the same way when a case just wouldn't jell. He headed to the coffee maker, setting about filling the carafe. "You could have helped yourself to coffee and food."

"I didn't want to wake you." She turned in her chair. "I already emailed my boss and the bank manager to ask about working remotely for the day. I'll let you know what they say."

"Good." He leaned against the counter as the coffee brewed. Joy had dressed for the office in a pink wool sweater, black dress pants, and a white blouse. Her blond hair was long and wavy, framing her cute face. She looked amazing, and it took him a minute to tear his gaze away to focus on the important matter of her safety. "It's probably best if you stay here to work."

She frowned. "Are you sure you want me to stay in your house without you?"

No, he wasn't sure of anything. But he felt certain his place was the safest place for Joy, at least for now. "Yeah, it's better than a hotel, right?"

"Right." She glanced at her computer, clicked the mouse, then frowned. "Although I guess that's not necessary. My request to work on the audit remotely was denied."

He straightened. "Why?"

"Security reasons." She grimaced. "It's not completely unexpected, I understand their reluctance. Even though I signed a nondisclosure and privacy agreement, the bank doesn't want their data on my laptop. And there's always a concern about introducing a virus to their network too."

He didn't like this, not one little bit. "Call in sick."

"I can't." She rose and crossed over to where he stood. "I'm not sick, and besides, I might learn something today. Someone may look surprised to see me alive and well."

He knew she meant it as a joke, but he didn't smile. Joy would be in danger the entire time she was in the Trustworthy Bank, and there was nothing he could do about it.

Except pray.

CHAPTER THREE

Tarin's concern warmed her heart, making her realize it had been a long time since anyone had worried about her welfare. Certainly not since she'd broken up with Kevin. Looking up into Tarin's warm brown eyes, she told herself not to read too much into his compassionate gaze.

His protective instincts were tied up in his profession as a cop. She wouldn't even be here if not for her desire to have him reopen her brother's case. Swallowing hard at the sudden awareness of his tall, muscular frame, she stepped to the side to reach for the coffeepot. Pulling it from the warmer, she reached up and snagged two mugs, pouring them each a cup.

Cradling the mug in her hands, grateful for the warmth, she offered an encouraging smile. "I'll be fine at the bank. It's not as if someone can sneak into the office to kill me."

"Anything is possible." His blunt words matched the serious expression on his face. He brushed his hand over his red hair, then took a sip of his coffee. "I'll make breakfast, then we'll head out. I'll want to see the space where you'll be working."

See the space? An office? In a bank? She frowned and tipped her head to the side. "Is that really necessary?"

"Yes." His tone didn't invite an argument.

"Suit yourself." She knew he would no matter what she said, so she let it go. "Do you need help with breakfast?"

"No, have a seat. This won't take long."

He looked so stern and serious, she reached over to rest her hand on his arm. "Tarin, I'm sure I'll be fine. There will be plenty of people around. It's a large bank with many different departments."

His gaze locked on hers with an intensity she'd never experienced before. She couldn't move, couldn't even breathe. She found herself wishing for something more, but then he looked away, breaking the moment.

"How do you like your eggs?" He set down his coffee and opened the fridge and pulled out a carton of eggs.

"I'll have whatever you like." She did her best to sound nonchalant, as if she hadn't almost thrown herself at him. Crossing over to the table, she sat in front of her computer. "I'm not picky."

"Over easy with toast?" He pulled out a fry pan and set it on the stove. Maybe she was imagining things, but he looked a bit distracted as he moved around the kitchen.

"Sounds good." She pushed the computer aside to make room. Tarin looked handsome in his suit coat and tie, his badge clipped to his belt. Along with his gun.

Her knowledge of police work mostly came from TV, except for the brief interactions she'd had with Tarin back when her brother had died. Five years ago, she'd been frustrated by the determination that Ken had killed himself. At the time, she hadn't really thought Tarin and his partner, Dave, had worked very hard to prove otherwise.

Yet the recent news about Dr. Eli Lewis's arrest had clearly sparked Tarin's interest.

Tarin made quick work of the meal, and as he had the night before, he bowed his head to pray. She'd never experienced a prayer before meals before. Based on how he didn't hesitate to do the blessing, she knew it was a normal routine for him.

"Lord, bless this food and please keep all of the Finnegans, and Joy too, safe in Your care. Amen."

"Amen." She was touched by the way he'd included her. "What was it like to grow up in such a large family?"

"Noisy, crazy, with absolutely no privacy, but also wonderful." The corner of his mouth kicked up in a small smile. "Hard to imagine growing up any other way, to be honest. I had a friend, Eric, in high school, and whenever I went to his house, it seemed so quiet. I remember wondering how he could stand being so alone all the time. Turns out, he wondered how I could stand being around people all day every day."

"Everyone adjusts to what they have, I guess." She took a bite of her eggs. "Thanks, this is great."

"They're nothing fancy." He was back to being his usual, quiet self. Maybe being one of nine meant he hadn't had to contribute much to the conversation around him.

When they'd finished eating, she stood with her plate. "I'll wash the dishes before we go."

"No need." He shook his head. "I'd rather get an early start. I'm supposed to report in by eight. I'll be pushing it to make that deadline as it is."

She was about to offer to take the bus, but deep down, she didn't want to. While the bank environment would be safe enough, the bus wouldn't.

Ten minutes later, they were ready to leave. After

shrugging into her winter coat, she gestured to her laptop. "Is it okay if I leave that here for now?"

"Sure, we'll need to swing by here later anyway. I plan to pick you up at the bank, so don't even think of leaving without me. Which reminds me, I need your phone number."

"I won't leave without you." She felt bad for interrupting his normal routine, but this wasn't the time to argue. She felt certain that after he'd checked out her office, he'd relax his guard a bit. And really, she should look at staying in a hotel closer to her work. That way, he wouldn't need to drive her back and forth.

She'd miss him, though, which was ridiculous since she barely knew him. Well, she knew Tarin prayed before meals, was the second oldest of nine, and was a fierce protector.

That was more than she knew about most of the people she worked with.

Other than exchanging phone numbers, Tarin was quiet on the drive to the Trustworthy Bank office in downtown Milwaukee. Maybe he found it as disconcerting to have his personal number as she did. The traffic wasn't terrible, but even so, she knew he'd be late for his shift. Parking was normally a nightmare, but Tarin pulled up directly in front of the building, setting a red police light on the dash.

"Is that legal?" she asked.

He flushed and shrugged. "It will do in a pinch. This shouldn't take too long."

They entered the lobby level of the bank. Tarin looked around, seeming to take it all in. Employees were making their way in, a group of them standing near the elevator.

"Do you eat lunch in that café?" Tarin gestured toward

the small café tucked in the corner of the lobby. The café also had a door leading outside to service the public too.

"Yes, why?" She frowned. "Trust me, it's very busy during the noon hour.

"Get your food and take it back up to your office," he advised. He escorted her to the group near the elevator. "And stay with others as much as possible."

"Okay." The elevator pinged. The group of people stepped inside, with her and Tarin going in last.

She was conscious of the curious stares boring into them, especially with Tarin's gun and badge visible between the open edges of his coat. No one stepped out on the second floor, which was the loan department. On the third floor, she stepped out with Tarin following close behind.

After going through the glass doors, she wound through the maze of cubicles to where her temporary office was located. Using her key, she unlocked the door and stepped inside. Turning, she caught more curious gazes, some with frank admiration as the women eyed Tarin.

"As you can see, I'm fine here." She slipped off her coat, surprised when he took it from her. "I—uh, there's a hook behind the door."

Tarin hung up her coat, then gazed around the small space, including the cubicles that could be seen through the glass door. "It's not as private as I imagined," he admitted.

"You better go, I feel bad making you late for work."

"Stay inside as much as possible and wait for me to call you before leaving for the day, okay?" He pinned her with a serious look. "Do not take any unnecessary chances."

"I won't." She set her purse on the desk, resisting the urge to hug him goodbye. As if the gossip mongers outside the office didn't have enough to talk about with her arriving with a man. "Take care, and please let me know what you find out."

He nodded, then surprised her by giving her a one-armed casual hug. "Stay safe," he murmured before turning and leaving the office. She couldn't tear her gaze away, watching as he retraced his steps through the cubicles back toward the elevator.

As soon as Tarin was gone, all gazes turned to her. She blushed and closed her office door, making it clear she wasn't interested in talking about it.

Besides, what could she say? She didn't want to mention the danger she was in or the details of the two shooting attempts.

She could pretend she and Tarin were dating, but that hardly seemed fair to him. He hadn't mentioned a girlfriend, and there was no evidence of female things at his home, but that didn't mean he wasn't seeing someone. In fact, she'd be surprised if a guy as good-looking as Tarin wasn't seeing someone.

The thought was depressing.

She sat down at her desk and booted up the computer. Time for her to stop thinking about Tarin Finnegan and to concentrate on her work.

As she logged in to the computer, she realized that the best way to figure out who had tried to shoot her was to get to the bottom of the data inconsistencies she'd found. Surely once she'd found and provided the information to her boss and the bank manager, she'd be off the hook and out of harm's way.

TARIN SLIPPED in behind the wheel of his SUV. As he drove to the precinct, he called his partner, Dave. "Hey, running late. Be there in fifteen."

"No problem. What's all this about two shooting incidents last night?"

Bad news traveled fast. "I'll fill you in when I get there. If you have time, I'd like you to dig into the credit card records of our latest vic, Kimberly Austin. I was going to do it last night, but the shooting incidents put a crimp in my plans."

"Will do," Dave agreed. They'd been partnered for five years now, but Tarin didn't have the same easy relationship with Dave as he'd had with Caroline. There wasn't any animosity, but Dave wasn't as much of a go-getter as Tarin would have expected.

There was no reason the guy couldn't figure out he needed to review the credit card information for himself. No, Tarin knew Dave had probably spent the past fifteen minutes drinking coffee and chatting with the other detectives instead of taking the initiative to dive into work.

Dave's laissez-faire attitude irked him, but there was no point in complaining about it. Their lieutenant would expect them to work it out. And when he toyed with the idea of asking for a new partner, in the end, he figured it was better to stick with someone he knew rather than take the risk with someone new.

Swallowing his frustration, he concentrated on navigating the streets. Thankfully, the impending storm that had been predicted had veered to the north, sparing them from dealing with two to four inches of the white stuff. Nothing could ruin a day's work faster than being stuck in traffic slowed to a crawl by snow.

When he finally arrived, he was waylaid by his lieutenant. "Finnegan? A moment."

He sighed and followed his boss into his office, not unlike the one Joy was working in on the other side of the city. He took a seat across from his boss's desk, trying not to feel like he was being called to the principal's office. "Hey, I don't know what you want me to say. It's not my fault I happened to be there when the idiot took shots at Joy Munson."

Lieutenant Gordon eyed him sullenly. "I'd buy that on the first attempt but not the second."

"Driving her home was the right thing to do," Tarin said evenly. "Especially after she was targeted outside Paulie's."

Gordon drummed his fingers on the desk. "You really think this is related to her work at the bank?"

"I don't know, I'm not the one investigating the case." Tarin suddenly straightened in his seat. "Unless you've decided to assign it to us? I'd be happy to dig into it—"

"No," Gordon interrupted. "You know better than to investigate a case in which you're a key witness. I'm just curious as to what your thoughts are on the issue."

"Boss, you know I don't form opinions until I've done the work." Tarin didn't like to go into any case with preconceived ideas. Which made him realize he'd failed to do that with Joy's brother's suicide. He'd been reeling from losing Caroline just two weeks earlier and had pretty much taken the scene that looked just like a suicide, verified by the ME's report, at face value.

"Yeah, yeah." Lieutenant Gordan waved an impatient hand. "I get it. You've got a good reputation for closing cases, Finnegan. Just take this as a warning not to interfere with the Munson shooting investigation, okay?"

He grimaced but nodded. "Is that all? I'd like to get cracking."

"That's all." Gordan turned to his computer.

Tarin stood and left the office, heading straight to the desk he shared with Dave Crowley. He took off his coat, draped it over the back of his chair, and took a seat. "Find anything?"

"In fifteen minutes? No." Dave didn't look over from the computer screen. "I'll let you know if something pops."

"Sure." Since Dave was going through the credit card statements, he turned his attention to poring through Kimberly Austin's social media accounts. They were waiting for the autopsy report to be completed, although when he'd gone to the ME's office yesterday to talk to the doc personally, he had only mentioned Kimberly had died of manual strangulation.

That much he'd figured out for himself.

"Hey, looks like our vic spent a lot of time at the Friendly Fitness Club, especially in the lounge/bar area." Dave turned to look at him. "She has charges there for the past four weeks before her murder."

"Good work. Her sisters claimed she wasn't dating anyone, but maybe she met her killer at the club. Could be the relationship was too new for her to talk about." He had to admit, it was a good clue. "We'll head back over to talk to the fitness club manager again but let me see if I can find any social media posts about the fitness center lounge."

Despite his desire to pull out Ken Munson's file, he knew the current murder victim had to take priority.

He found a picture of their vic with a guy wearing a tank top and bulging muscles with a pool in the background. He printed it out and grabbed his coat. "Let's go. This might be our guy."

The next ninety minutes passed quickly. The interview at the Friendly Fitness Club revealed the guy in the picture was Vance Silva, who admitted to seeing Kimberly. At first he voluntarily came in for questioning, even admitting he was with Kimberly earlier on the day she died, but when they asked him outright if he'd killed her, Vance lashed out in anger. He pounded his open palms on the table and screamed for a lawyer. While Dave ushered him out of the room, Tarin asked one of the CSIs to lift his fingerprints from the metal table.

"Quite the temper on that guy," Dave said as they reconvened at their desks. "Easy to imagine him losing control and strangling Kimberly."

"Yeah, maybe. I'll call the lab, see if they've lifted fingerprints from the vic's neck. If we can get even a partial match to those we have from today, we'll charge him."

An hour later, they had their match. Confronted with the evidence, Vance and his lawyer cut a deal with the DA's office to plead manslaughter as he'd killed Kimberly in a fit of rage when she'd declined to see him anymore. Apparently, Vance also used steroids, which may have contributed to the crime. Either way, they'd closed the case, which was a good feeling. After tasking Dave with writing up the report, Tarin retrieved the file on Ken Munson.

As he read through it again, he inwardly cringed at his lack of detail. Sure, he could blame it on Caroline's death, but he should have taken more time off rather than muddling through and possibly bungling a case.

He had noted the name of the doc on the empty prescription bottle found on the floor beside Ken's bed. The name Dr. Eli Lewis was clear on the photograph he'd included in the report too.

There was no sign of the pharmacist name, though, and

that was something he should not have overlooked. Glancing at the clock, he saw the time was eleven fifteen. He decided to meet Joy for lunch at the café in her bank building, to see if she could fill him in on what he may have missed in the initial investigation.

Not that he should have missed anything five years ago. His failure nagged at him as he glanced at his partner. "Thanks for doing the report."

"No problem," Dave said with a shrug. "Should we look at some of our other open cases?"

"This afternoon. I—uh, need to take some time off for lunch." Tarin hadn't told his partner about his intent to reopen the Ken Munson file. "If you don't mind."

"Doesn't matter to me." Dave continued typing on the computer.

"Finnegan, call on line two," someone shouted.

Tarin picked up the phone. "Detective Finnegan, can I help you?"

"Hey, this is Banfield, from the Brookland PD. I wanted you to know the slugs we pulled out of the vic's door were too mangled for a ballistics match."

Tarin swallowed a groan, he'd been afraid of that. "Thanks for letting me know. What about the canvass of the area? Did anyone else see a dark, silent sedan driving by?"

"Nope. We still have a few houses to hit, but it's not looking good," Banfield admitted. "Sorry I don't have better news."

"Not your fault." Tarin wished he could see the evidence for himself but refrained from asking. Banfield was being nice enough to fill him in, which he appreciated. "Thanks for all your help on this, Officer Banfield."

"I'll let you know if we find something new," the officer promised. "Later."

"Bye." Tarin dropped the receiver into the cradle and reached for his coat. "I'll be back in an hour."

"That's fine." Dave shrugged. "I'll take a look at our other open cases and see what we can dig into next."

"Thanks." He knew there was also the possibility of getting another call to head out to a fresh crime scene, so he needed to make this quick. The sooner he could ask Joy about the name of the pharmacist who was overseeing Ken's work as a resident, the better.

Hurrying down to the parking lot, he squelched a flash of anticipation. No matter how attractive he found Joy, this would be a work meeting not a lunch date. The stern lecture did not dampen his desire to get to the bank building as quickly as possible.

Idiot, he muttered to himself. His fault for hugging her when he'd left her office. He'd intended it to be a friendly gesture. Yet there was no denying he'd wanted more.

That was impossible, not to mention inappropriate, so he thrust that idea right out of his mind. The sky was full of darkening clouds, making the day seem later than it was. Maybe the snow would make an appearance after all. In his years of working homicide, a snowstorm was the only thing that seemed to deter crime. Apparently, even the bad guys didn't want to run around in the snow.

Worked for him.

This time, he decided against parking in front of the bank building. No sense in pushing his luck, especially in the middle of the day. Besides, he wouldn't mind walking around the lobby for a bit since it wasn't quite noon.

Muttering under his breath, Tarin drove around for a full ten minutes before finding a parking spot four blocks away. He used his phone app to pay the meter, then strode quickly toward the bank building.

It occurred to him he should call Joy to let her know he was coming. With one hand, he scrolled through his contacts until he found her name, then pushed the button to call her.

After several rings, the call went to her voice mail.

He frowned and tucked his phone into his coat pocket. Was she in the middle of a meeting? Or was there some other reason she hadn't responded? He quickened his pace, resisting the urge to call her again and again until she answered the phone.

There had been lots of people in the office area around her. Earlier, he'd found the environment somewhat reassuring. Having people around would normally deter a gunman, especially one that had waited to strike at night.

Still, he pushed through some pedestrians in his haste to get inside the building. He stood in the lobby for a moment, scanning the area for Joy's familiar blond hair.

There were a couple of blond females but none wearing a pink wool sweater. Crossing the linoleum floor, he went into the small and crowded café.

It didn't take long to confirm Joy wasn't there either. Relaxing a bit, he went back to the open lobby and called her phone again.

No answer.

His jaw clenched, and he strode to the elevator, hitting the button harder than necessary. The elevator was coming down from the tenth floor, seeming to stop at every single level on the way down.

He stepped back when the elevator reached the lobby, anticipating it would be full of people. And it was. Several people stepped out, including Joy.

"Joy!" He waved to get her attention.

"Tarin?" Her eyes widened in shock. "What on earth are you doing here?"

"I was hoping to talk to you." He felt a little foolish now for worrying about her safety. "I called you a few times, hoping you'd come meet me for lunch."

"Oh, sorry." She flushed. "I must have left my phone on silent." She pulled it from her purse. "I was doing as you suggested, waiting around for several of the other employees to come down for lunch, too, so I wouldn't be alone."

"I'm glad." He shouldn't have overreacted, although in his defense, someone had taken shots at her twice in one night. "Let's get something to eat and find a spot where we can talk for a few minutes."

"Is this about the shooting incidents?" she asked in a low voice so no one else would overhear.

"No, unfortunately, I don't have anything new to share about that. I wanted to ask you about your brother's work at the pharmacy." He opened the café door for her so they could get in line. Several of the people who'd been in the elevator with Joy were there, but others had gone outside, presumably to get their meals elsewhere.

"Okay." She looked happy to hear he'd opened her brother's case. The line moved quickly, and soon they'd placed their sandwich orders. She reached for her purse, but he waved it away, paying for her meal despite her protest.

"It's the least I can do." He felt bad about the way he'd handled her brother's case. When a table right next to the window overlooking the street opened, he quickly snagged it. Talking about the case in a crowded space wasn't ideal, but he highly doubted anyone would be able to listen to their conversation above the din.

He scooted his chair closer to hers and took her hand.

They didn't have a lot of time, so he made it a quick blessing. "Lord, we ask You to bless our food. Amen," he whispered.

"Amen," she echoed.

As he unwrapped his meal, he asked, "I looked over the reports I'd made of your brother's death."

"Thanks for doing that." She took a bite of her sandwich.

They ate in silence for a few moments, before he said, "I hate to admit this, but I neglected to document the name of the pharmacist he was working for. You mentioned Ken was a resident, so he wasn't working on his own, correct?"

"Yes, that's right. His supervising pharmacist was Craig Washington." She leaned closer to him. "You think he might be involved in this?"

"I don't know, but I need to check him out." The way he should have five years ago.

A loud crack echoed loudly as glass shards rained upon them. "Down!" he croaked, tucking Joy's head down so he could cover her with his body.

The shooter had struck again!

CHAPTER FOUR

With her face down and pressed against Tarin's chest, Joy couldn't see what was happening. But she could hear the shouts, screams, and the sound of running feet crunching on shards of glass as customers fled the café.

She swallowed hard as Tarin called for backup. Then he slid off his chair, tugging her over with him.

"We need to stay down." He gently shoved her beneath the table. "Help is on the way."

"Why does this keep happening?" The question was stupid because Tarin didn't know any more than she did. Her mind just couldn't seem to grapple with the third attempt against her, and in broad daylight no less.

"I wish I knew." Tarin's voice was grim. He hadn't joined her under the table. From her position, she couldn't see him very well, other than he was on his knees beside her, weapon in hand.

Less than a minute later, sirens wailed, growing louder as they approached the bank building. It was then she realized she wouldn't be able to go back to work. They wouldn't want her there, not after this.

And maybe that was exactly what the shooter had intended. To scare her into giving up her job. After all, what kind of a killer missed his target three times?

"I'm inside the café with the target. We're sheltering in place until you arrive." Tarin must have been talking to someone on his phone. "Yeah, I see you now. Go ahead and send in the team."

More footsteps crunching on glass as several officers surrounded the table. Tarin held out his hand. She took it, allowing him to draw her from the hiding spot.

The cops around them were dressed in what looked like bullet-resistant vests and helmets. A tall blond-haired man crossed over to Tarin. "You okay, bro?"

"Yeah, but this is the third attempt against Joy, er Ms. Munson," Tarin said. "Gotta tell you, Rhy, I don't like it. This guy took a shot in the middle of the day!"

"Captain Finnegan?" another voice called. "We have the café surrounded, no sign of the shooter yet."

"Understood, but we need to keep searching, and I want officers canvassing the area," Rhy replied. Joy realized the tall blond man was one of Tarin's five brothers. Tarin's hair was red, but they shared similar facial features and the same brown eyes. She shouldn't have been surprised to learn he was a cop, too, holding the rank of captain. Tarin's jacket and tie looked out of place among the other cops, yet they treated him as one of their own.

His badge was gold rather than silver, but it was still a badge.

"We need to find the slug." Tarin glanced around the small space. After a moment, he saw something and moved away to check it out. Joy missed his warm presence and shivered a bit with the cold air flowing freely through the broken window.

Rhy followed his brother, so she trailed along too. When she saw the bullet embedded in the wall, much the way they'd been stuck in her front door, she battled a wave of anger.

Why was this guy doing this? She was no threat to anyone! Except maybe the bank employee responsible for the irregularities she'd found in her audit. Unfortunately, she was no closer to getting to the bottom of who was responsible.

If they took her off the case, she'd never know.

The anger faded, replaced by a bone-deep weariness. This gunman would get what he wanted. She'd leave, and someone else would take over.

That would put a stop to all this craziness. And in truth, at this point, she didn't even care who was responsible.

She just wanted to feel safe. Which didn't seem like too much to ask.

"The Brookland PD said the bullets taken from Joy's front door were too demolished to be tested for forensics," Tarin said as an officer carefully pried the slug from the drywall. "Maybe this one will offer more."

"Looks like it's in decent shape." The cop dropped the bullet fragment into an evidence bag. "Going through the glass may have slowed it enough that it didn't become as damaged."

"Or the perp took the shot from farther away." Tarin turned to stare at the damaged window. He took out his phone and pushed a button to provide a laser type of light. Positioning the phone where the bullet was, he lined it up with the window.

The blood drained from her face when she realized how close the bullet had come to hitting her in the head. Much like the previous attempts, the bullet had only missed her by a fraction of an inch.

Okay, maybe this attempt and the others weren't just meant to scare her. Maybe this guy really wanted her dead.

But why? That was the real conundrum. Killing her wouldn't put an end to the audit.

Unless they had bribed some other accountant to look the other way when that person stepped in to take over.

It seemed as if she'd been dropped in the center of a horror movie set. Only the blood was real.

Blood? She looked down at her pretty white blouse and pink sweater, realizing both were stained red. She put a hand to the side of her neck. A shard of glass was embedded in the skin beneath her ear.

With trembling fingers, she removed the glass, dropping it onto the floor. She looked around, found some napkins, and used them to wipe the blood from her hands, then pressed one to the cut on her neck. It stung, but from what she could tell without a mirror, it wasn't too deep.

"The ambulance is outside, we'll get you checked out soon," Tarin said, noticing her actions.

"I'm fine." Her voice lacked conviction because she was far from okay. The wound was nothing, but her entire life was in shambles.

"This way." Tarin put his arm around her shoulders and steered her toward the lobby. Two EMTs were coming toward her, pushing a gurney topped with medical supplies. "Please have a seat, here, and let them examine you."

She collapsed onto the chair, mostly because her legs wouldn't hold her weight another second longer. Resisting the urge to bury her face in her hands and cry, she sat perfectly straight as the female EMT looked at her wound.

"It's not deep, should only need a couple of stitches," she said.

"Stitches?" She recoiled from the idea. "Can't you just put a bandage on it?"

"You don't want it to leave a scar," the woman said. "It won't hurt, they'll numb up your skin so you won't feel a thing."

A scar was the least of her worries. You had to be alive to notice a scar. A rush of paranoia hit hard, and she looked frantically around at the sea of strangers. What if the gunman was right here, watching her? Getting some weird kick of excitement from of the chaos he'd created?

"Just put a bandage over it." She couldn't hide the hint of desperation in her tone. "I'm not going to the hospital for stitches. I want to go home."

"Okay, that's fine. I'll need you to sign a release form, though." The two EMTs looked at her with sympathy, but they didn't know a fraction of the story. That this was the third time in less than twenty-four hours that she'd almost been killed by gunfire.

The moment the dressing had been applied, she signed their stupid paper, then pushed herself upright. Skirting around them, she went to find Tarin. He was in deep conversation with his brother, no doubt still discussing the recent shooting.

She put a hand on Tarin's arm to interrupt. "I'm sorry, but I really need to get out of here."

Rhy arched a brow. "And go where?"

"She's been staying at my place." Rhy's brow arched even higher, making Tarin scowl. "Don't lecture me. It was only a few weeks ago that you brought a stranger to the homestead. At least I didn't expose our siblings to danger."

"Hey, Devon is my fiancée not a stranger." Rhy's wry

grin faded. "Are you sure you and Joy are safe at your house?"

"Safer than here." Tarin shrugged. "It's temporary, until we can figure out where the threat is coming from."

She didn't like being discussed as if she wasn't standing right there. "I want to leave," she repeated, wincing at how she sounded like a petulant child. "Please," she added, softly. "I don't feel safe here."

Tarin's stern expression softened. "Okay, I'll take you to my place. Rhy, will you please let me know if you find anything else?"

"Will do." Rhy glanced at her, looking as if he might say something, but he turned away, instead raising his voice to address the team of cops still in the area. "What's the update from the canvass? Any witnesses?"

"Do you want to go upstairs to get your coat?" Tarin asked.

She nodded. "If you don't mind. I need to let the bank manager know I'm leaving too."

Tarin escorted her to the elevator and up to the third floor. She quickly grabbed her coat from the hook behind the door, then poked her head into the bank manager's office. He wasn't there, probably at lunch, so she turned away. "I'll have to send him an email."

"You can do that from my place. Ready to get out of here?" Tarin asked, holding her coat for her so she could slip into it. "I'd bring my SUV up so you wouldn't have to walk, but they have the roads blocked off. Can you make it four blocks?"

"Yes, I'm not an invalid." Walking four blocks was nothing but a minor inconvenience compared to staying here. She'd have gladly gone much farther if necessary. After taking the elevator down to the lobby, she and Tarin headed outside. Ominous dark clouds swirled overhead, adding to the grim atmosphere. There were plenty of squads and cops in the area, but her earlier paranoia wouldn't leave her alone.

Shivering from cold and fear, she huddled close to Tarin as he led them to the parking spot where he'd left his SUV. It wasn't until they were seated inside and Tarin was driving away that she began to feel safe.

For now.

"I know Rhy is one of your five brothers," she said, breaking the silence. "Is he older or younger?"

"Rhy is the oldest. I'm next, then we have Kyleigh, Brady, Quinn, Colin, Aiden, Alanna, and Elly. Oh, and Aiden and Alanna are twins."

The names whirled in her mind, but she tried to stay focused on Tarin and Rhy, the two she'd met. "Sounds nice."

"Most of the time." He shot her a glance. "I'm sorry about this, Joy. I knew you going to work was a risk, but I honestly didn't expect this guy to shoot in the middle of the day. I figured he'd use the early morning or late afternoon hours if he was going to try again."

"You're not to blame." A wave of weariness washed over her. "I'm just glad you were with me."

"Me too." Tarin reached over to take her hand. She gripped his warm fingers, desperately wishing she never had to let him go.

THREE STRIKES, *you're out*, Tarin thought grimly as he took a circuitous route to his place. He was so engrossed in the shooting event he'd totally forgotten about Dave waiting for him back at the precinct.

Letting go of Joy's hand wasn't an option. He needed the physical connection and wasn't ready to release it. These attempts against her were really starting to make him angry. And for a moment, he wondered if maybe he'd been the target.

After all, all three shooting incidents had happened when they were together.

But no, that didn't really make sense either. Sure, he'd put many bad guys behind bars, several who'd threatened to seek revenge, but he'd been alone several times over the past twenty-four hours. He'd walked to Paulie's alone, had walked the four blocks to the bank alone. The perp hadn't shown up at his house either. Not that he advertised where he lived, but a criminal with connections could easily find that information out by doing a property search under his name.

The thought sent a chill down his spine, so he took another series of turns, backtracking to triple-check he wasn't being followed.

Forty minutes later, he pulled into his driveway. He parked in the garage, closing the door right away so that it wouldn't look as if anyone was there. Releasing Joy's hand, he slid out from behind the wheel, making sure to grab Ken Munson's file. Inside the house, he set the file on the table and faced Joy. "We never had a chance to finish eating. I can whip up some sandwiches if you like."

"No thanks, I'm not hungry." She frowned, looking down at her blood-stained clothes. "If you don't mind, I'd like to take a shower and change."

"What about your dressing?" He should have insisted

she go to the hospital. "There's still time to go in for stitches."

"I'd rather not." She looked so dejected and exhausted he didn't have the heart to force the issue.

"Okay, I have a first aid kit. I'll change the dressing for you after you're finished." On this, he stood firm. "Best to keep it clean, right?"

She nodded and slipped down the hall toward the guest room. His phone rang, and he sighed when he saw Dave's number.

"Where are you?" His partner sounded cranky.

"Sorry, I was at the scene of the shooting, you know, at the Trustworthy Bank building?"

"Why didn't you call me to come with you?"

His partner assumed he'd been called in as the detective assigned to the case. "I was a witness, Dave, I was having lunch with the victim of the previous incidents."

"You were having lunch. With a victim." Dave repeated the words with sarcasm. "Are you nuts? You can't do that."

"Remember that suicide we investigated? It was our first case together. Vic's name was Ken Munson."

"I remember, although it was an open-and-shut case. ME called it suicide, and the evidence we found at the scene supported that." Dave sounded impatient. "What of it?"

"Joy Munson is Ken's sister. The doctor's name on the prescription bottle we found in Ken's bedroom is Eli Lewis. He was recently arrested for selling drugs using fake prescriptions. Upward of five million dollars was found in offshore accounts."

"Okay, so the prescription is fake, but that doesn't mean Ken didn't kill himself," Dave argued.

"Could be Ken's death was set up to look like a suicide

because he stumbled onto the drug scheme." He'd wanted to have this conversation with his partner face-to-face so he could see the expression in Dave's eyes. "I think it's worth digging a little deeper, to make sure we didn't miss anything."

"We have enough to do without wasting time digging into closed cases," Dave scoffed. "Besides, that doesn't explain why you're not here."

"Jo—er, Ms. Munson is an accountant. She was hired to do a bank audit at Trustworthy Bank and has found some irregularities. Someone has tried to kill her three times now, this last attempt in the lobby café of the bank itself. I had to drive her someplace safe."

"You could have gotten a patrol officer to do it," Dave pointed out.

"Yeah, well, I don't like the way she's being used for target practice." He feared it was only a matter of time until the bullet hit its mark. The injury below her ear was from glass, but if she'd been struck there, the bullet would have severed her spinal cord.

Thanks to Alanna being a nurse and his brother Colin being a paramedic firefighter, not to mention his own stint as a homicide detective, he knew far more than he ever wanted to about traumatic injuries.

And the idea of losing Joy filled him with a horrified dread. No way could he allow that to happen.

"So, you'll be in when?" Dave was growing impatient with the conversation. "Soon?"

His original intent had been to leave Joy here to head back to the precinct, but now that he was here, he knew that wasn't an option. No way was he about to leave her here alone. "No. I need to take the rest of the day off."

"Really?" Dave sounded surprised.

"Yeah, sorry. I have some things I need to do."

His partner paused, then said, "Okay, whatever. I pulled the Connor Patton file, I'll work on that while you're gone."

"Thanks, Dave, that's a good one to work on." Connor Patton had been killed in a drive-by shooting thirty-six hours ago. The trail had quickly gone cold, mostly because no one claimed to have seen anything, and the vehicle identified via a traffic camera was stolen. "I still think we'll find the car soon, maybe keep checking with the towing companies. I'm sure one of them scooped it up."

"Will do." If Dave was irritated at being told what to do, he hid it well. "Let me know if you need anything."

"I will, thanks again." He ended the call, hoping that searching for the stolen vehicle would keep his partner occupied for the rest of the afternoon.

Tarin called Lieutenant Gordon next, asking for personal time off for the rest of the day and possibly for the following day too. Since he'd never taken a sick day or personal time since losing Caroline, his boss readily agreed. Then Gordon added, "Finnegan, is everything okay? It's not like you to duck out like this."

"I know, sorry about that. I just have some personal things to do."

"That's fine but keep in touch." He could tell his boss was not reassured. But he didn't care. He had bigger issues to worry about.

"I will, thanks again." After disconnecting from the line, he tapped his phone in the palm of his hand, wondering why he hadn't taken the opportunity to discuss his plan to reopen the Ken Munson case. Sure, his boss would have given him a hard time, but in the end, the lieutenant usually let his detectives follow their gut instincts.

Of course, it helped that Rhy was on the job, too, as a captain over the tactical teams. The Finnegan name meant something to the upper brass, and he appreciated that he didn't get ridden too hard by Gordon.

A situation that would change on a dime if the lieutenant knew he had the victim of three shootings staying in his home.

He blew out a heavy sigh and headed to his room to change out of his dress clothes. After donning a police sweatshirt and jeans, he returned to the kitchen to make a pot of coffee. He needed to fill in more of the blanks in Ken Munson's file, and he found it easier to concentrate with a cup of coffee next to him. While that was brewing, he waited until Joy finished in the bathroom to grab the first aid kit Alanna had given to him. Well, she'd provided one to each sibling the year she'd graduated from college with her bachelor's degree in Nursing. At first they'd joked about it, but over time they'd each had the opportunity to use it.

At the table, he drank coffee and made notes on a sheet of paper. He added the name Craig Washington as the pharmacist overseeing Ken's work. The last name was very common, but he'd enter it into their database to see if he was able to get any hits on the guy.

It would be interesting if both Washington and Lewis had been arrested. That would surely be enough to convince the upper brass they needed to reinvestigate the case.

Where was Joy? He wanted to ask a few more questions, but she hadn't come out of her room yet. After checking his watch for the tenth time in ten minutes, he rose and padded down the hall. Her door was closed, and while she obviously deserved privacy, he lightly rapped on it. "Joy? Are you okay?"

"Yes." Her voice was muffled, making it hard to tell if she was crying.

"Joy, please. Come out and talk to me." He hated to think of her suffering in silence. This situation was a lot for anyone to deal with, especially a woman who spent her time poring over data-filled spreadsheets.

About as far from street crime as a person could get.

He waited, but she didn't say anything more. He knew from having three sisters that sometimes giving them space was what they needed. Even though he didn't like knowing she was upset, he turned away.

Then he heard rustling and the door opening. Turning to face her, his heart squeezed painfully at her puffy red eyes. "I'm sorry," she began, but he simply shook his head and drew her into his arms.

"Don't apologize. This is not your fault." He tucked her head beneath his chin and cradled her close, the way he'd done with Elly when she was sixteen and melting down after her boyfriend broke up with her.

This was far more serious, of course. Joy's life was in danger, and they really had very little to go on.

"I don't know why I'm overreacting," she murmured against his chest. "Logically, I know I'm safe here with you."

"I promise no one will hurt you while I'm here," he reassured her. "But you have a right to be upset. You've been through a lot over the past eighteen hours."

He felt her take in a long, deep breath, letting it out slowly. He continued holding her until she eased away, lifting her head to look up at him. "Thanks, Tarin. I wouldn't be here at all if not for you."

"Hey, my job is to protect innocent people from bad guys." He strove for a light tone but couldn't tear his gaze from her sweet mouth. He'd never wanted to kiss anyone as badly as he wanted to kiss Joy.

But she needed a friendly shoulder, not a kiss. He tried to smile. "Why don't you let me bandage that wound for you?"

"Okay. Although when I looked at it in the mirror, it wasn't nearly as bad as I thought when I saw all the blood."

"It's still important to keep it covered." He could almost hear Alanna's voice lecturing him in his mind. He eased back a step. "The first aid kit is in the kitchen."

She nodded and pulled out of his embrace. Giving himself a mental shake along with a stern warning to stay focused, he followed her into the kitchen.

"Have a seat." He gestured to the chair next to the first aid kit.

Rather than sitting down, she turned to face him. "Do you mind if I ask you a personal question?"

"Of course not, what is it?" He tried to read her gaze.

"Is there someone in your life who will be upset to know I'm staying here?" It was a roundabout way of asking if he had a girlfriend.

"No, I'm not involved with anyone." He wasn't sure why she'd asked, until she stepped closer and lifted herself up on her toes to kiss him.

The friendly vibe he'd been striving to maintain vanished in a nanosecond, replaced by a hot rush of desire.

And he knew in that instant he was in deep, deep trouble.

CHAPTER FIVE

Kissing Tarin was probably a mistake, but Joy didn't care. After being so close to death over the past several hours, she needed this.

Needed to feel alive.

Yet, as amazing as his embrace was, she could feel him pulling away. With reluctance, she broke off the kiss, leaning back to look into his eyes. "Thanks, Tarin."

He looked adorably confused. "For what?"

"For being right here when I needed you the most." She rested her hand in the center of his chest, on the MPD police emblem embossed on his dark-blue sweatshirt. "I treasure your support. Especially now." She tried to downplay the kiss. "I shouldn't have overstepped, but it's been a long day, and it's only half over."

"I—uh, you don't have to apologize." He glanced around the kitchen as if forgetting what he'd been about to do. "Ah, we need to dress that wound."

"All right." She took pity on him, stepping away and dropping into the closest chair.

Tarin took his time rummaging through the kit, then

went down onto his knee to access the spot beneath her ear better. She breathed in his unique scent, wishing for something she couldn't have.

Oh, he'd responded to their kiss, but that alone didn't mean much. She didn't doubt he looked at her like one of his sisters.

"Tell me about your family," she said as he applied antibiotic ointment to the cut. "I know you listed their names, but what do your siblings do for work?"

"We're all first responders to a certain extent. You met Rhy; we both work for the Milwaukee Police Department. Kyleigh is a Milwaukee County Sheriff's deputy stationed at the courthouse. Brady is an FBI agent, Quinn is with the Coast Guard, Colin is a firefighter/paramedic, Aiden is with the National Guard full time, Alanna is an ER nurse, and Elly is training to be an EMT." He paused, looking thoughtful, then added, "Yeah, I think that's everyone."

"Sounds like your family is very focused on community service."

"Our dad was a cop, and our mom was a nurse. We followed their example." He finished taping a small dressing over the cut, then quickly stood.

"Are they both retired now?"

He shook his head. "Our parents died ten years ago. Me and Rhy moved back home to keep the siblings together. Elly is twelve years younger than Rhy, she was only fourteen when we lost our parents, and the twins were seventeen. Colin and Quinn were both still at home back then too."

"That was a very honorable thing to do." She searched his gaze. "I'm sure that wasn't easy, though."

He shrugged as he repacked the first aid kit. "Rhy is the one who took charge, I filled the role of his wingman."

She imagined Tarin was an awesome wingman. And hearing what he and Rhy had done, basically putting their own personal lives on hold to keep the family together, only reinforced her original thought that his concern for her was nothing special. He would do the same thing for anyone in her situation.

Okay, then, she'd take care not to cross the line again. No matter how tempting he was. "I guess we should talk about Ken's death."

"Yes, I would like for you to fill in more blanks if you can." He left the room with the first aid kit, returning a moment later. "I need to apologize for the lack of detail five years ago. I don't have an excuse, other than I'd lost my partner, Caroline, two weeks before I was assigned to your brother's case. I had taken some time off, but looking back, maybe I should have been off work longer." He sat beside her at the table, his expression full of self-recrimination. "I wasn't as thorough as I should have been."

The way he mentioned his partner, Caroline, gave her pause. Were they more than work partners? It shouldn't matter, but she felt the pang of jealously just the same. "It's okay, Tarin. I doubt taking down these additional details would have changed the outcome of the investigation."

"Probably not, but it's still inexcusable." He stared down at his notepad. "You and your brother deserved better."

"Hey, we have new information now, right?" She hated to see him beat himself up over something that wasn't his fault. "That's what matters."

"Yeah." He picked up his pen and glanced at her. "Tell me what you know about the pharmacy. I remember it wasn't one of those large chain pharmacies but independently owned and operated, right?"

"Yes. Ken mentioned Craig Washington owned the pharmacy, doing most of the work himself. But he was looking for additional help, which was why he'd partnered with the University of Madison School of Pharmacy to take on a pharmacy resident. Ken was excited to have the opportunity, especially since Craig made it sound like Ken would be able to have a job there after he took his boards."

"Interesting." Tarin made more notes on his legal pad. "Did other employees work there? From what I know of pharmacies, they always have a tech or someone to help manage stock."

"Yes, there were two pharmacy techs." She frowned, trying to remember what Ken had talked about back then. "I can't remember their names, though."

"That's okay, I may be able to figure it out." Tarin made another note. "I looked, and the pharmacy is still in business, so I'll swing by to talk to the staff."

Her stomach clenched at the thought of being here alone, but she didn't voice her concern. After all, she was the one who'd asked Tarin to reopen her brother's case. She was safe enough here.

But for how long? She couldn't assume he'd want her to stick around indefinitely. Her original plan was to get a hotel room close to the Trustworthy Bank office building, but that wasn't a priority now.

"I—uh, we should look for a hotel too." She cleared her throat. "You mentioned my staying here was a short-term arrangement."

"That was before the third incident of gunfire." He frowned. "Would you rather stay in a hotel?"

"No, I wouldn't." She couldn't lie. "I know it's an inconvenience for you, but I'd rather stay in your guest room for another night."

"It's easier for me if you stay here," Tarin admitted ruefully. "I won't leave you alone, Joy. If you really want to go to a hotel, I'll go with you."

"That's very sweet, but we may as well stay here, then." She couldn't hide her relief. "Thanks for allowing me to stay. I wish I understood why this guy wants me dead."

"That reminds me, did you talk to your boss?"

"Yes. I filled him in on the three attempts to shoot me, and he agreed to allowing me to take a personal leave of absence from work." He'd done so grudgingly and had limited her time off to two weeks maximum. "However, he doesn't think the shootings are related to my work at the bank."

"Why not?" Tarin demanded with a dark scowl. "It's the most logical motive."

"Yes, but as I mentioned before, they'll just send another accountant to take my place." She spread her hands. "I guess we can see what happens when Benjamin steps in to do the audit. If no one goes after him, then we'll know the bank staff aren't involved."

"What's Benjamin's last name?" Tarin drew a line across the page. "And what do you know about him?"

"Benjamin Adler, he's been with the firm for six years. I have more seniority, though, as I've been there ten years." She flushed. "I'm only thirty-three, but I started college early and took the CPA exam when I was twenty-three."

"Impressive." Tarin took more notes. "What else do you know about Adler?"

"He's married, has a young child, I think Carly is two years old now." She cocked her head. "You think he's involved in this?"

"I'm simply gathering information, but anything is possible."

"There's no reason on earth for Ben to do something like this. Scare me off just so he could take over the audit? And do what? Take a bribe to make sure the results come back clean?"

"I've seen worse things done for less motive." Tarin grimaced. "I'm sorry, Joy, but it's my nature to look for the worst in people."

"That must be a sad way to live."

His gaze caught hers. "Sometimes, yes. But right now, there's nothing more important than your safety. And if that means poking my nose into other people's personal lives, then that's just too bad."

A warm glow washed over her at his words. Logically, she knew Tarin was being nice, that as a cop, of course, he took protecting the public seriously.

But she appreciated his steely determination to watch over her more than she could say. Tarin's actions only reinforced she was better off without Kevin Creek.

It also made her realize that no man she'd ever known came close to being as warm, protective, and caring as Tarin Finnegan. He would be difficult, if not impossible, to replace.

A wave of sadness and regret hit hard. As much as she wanted the danger to be over, she knew that once this mystery was solved, she wouldn't see Tarin again.

KISSING JOY HAD KNOCKED him seriously off-balance in a way he hadn't experienced in a long time. Even now, when he was doing his best to have a normal and professional conversation with her about her brother's death, he wanted to kiss her again.

Was this what Rhy had gone through with Devon last month? His older brother had brought a woman who was in danger to the Finnegan homestead, only to fall in love with her. Rhy and Devon were engaged and scheduled to get married next month. Truly, he was happy for Rhy. He certainly deserved to have a family of his own, especially after everything Rhy had sacrificed to keep the Finnegan siblings together.

Still, he was not interested in following his brother's path. He'd loved Caroline, and losing her had gutted him. He was okay with his life; he didn't need to get tangled up with a woman. No matter how beautiful or sweet. Best for him to remember that Joy Munson was off-limits.

No more kissing or hugging or any of that personal stuff, he told himself sternly. He'd maintain a professional demeanor from now on.

Deep down, he could secretly admit that would be easier said than done.

He and Joy worked on her brother's case for the next thirty minutes. When his stomach growled loud enough for her to hear it, she jumped to her feet.

"I'll warm up that leftover hamburger for you since you didn't get to finish your lunch."

"I can do it," he offered, but she shook her head.

"Please, I'd like to do something useful." She crossed to the fridge and pulled out the leftovers.

For a moment, he remembered Rhy's fiancée, Devon, doing something similar. Doing her part to help with the chores while staying at the homestead. The similarities between the two situations were impossible to ignore. Yet that didn't mean they had to end the same way.

In fact, Tarin was convinced they wouldn't. He cared about Joy the way he would any woman who'd been targeted by gunfire by an escalating perp three times in less than twenty-four hours. But their personal lives were vastly different.

When Rhy had announced his engagement to the family at Sunday dinner, Tarin had later warned him that not every woman was cut out to be a cop's wife. The divorce rate among police officers was high; the stress of the job took its toll.

But Rhy had reminded Tarin that with faith and God's love, anything was possible. No way to argue that, so he'd let it go. Especially since he really liked Devon, and he especially appreciated how she made Rhy happy.

He continued reviewing his notes, outlining a plan to pick up the threads of the investigation until Joy set a plate in front of him. Pushing the notepad aside, he glanced up at her. "You remembered exactly how I liked it."

She flushed and nodded. "I tend to be detail-oriented."

"Good quality for a CPA," he joked. "Are you sure you're not hungry? There's plenty of food in the fridge, feel free to help yourself."

"I'm fine." She dropped into the chair beside him.

He bowed his head, offering a silent prayer of thanks before picking up his burger. He felt better after taking a few bites. His body was strange that way, he didn't function as well on an empty stomach. "This is great, thanks."

"It's your food," she said. "What's next?"

He thought about that for a moment. First, he wanted an update from the crime scene at the bank. He doubted they had much to share, or they'd have reached out. Then he wanted to head over to the pharmacy owned by Craig Washington. It was called Craig's Corner Pharmacy and was advertised as an independent pharmacy offering the lowest prices in the city. *Like anyone would advertise the highest prices*, he thought.

How a small pharmacy like Craig's Corner competed with the big guys like CVS and Walgreens was a mystery. Unless, of course, Craig had something going on the side with doctors like Eli Lewis.

He took a sip of his coffee. "I'd like to pay Craig's Corner a visit."

"Can I ride along?" She flushed, then added, "I can wait in the car if that would make you feel better."

Bringing her along wasn't part of the plan, but he took a moment to reconsider. Rather than going in as a detective, they may get more information from a casual conversation. "Yeah, you can come along. It might work to our advantage if you strike up a conversation with the employees about your brother."

"I can do that." She brightened. "I'll mention that I've been thinking about Ken since the five-year anniversary of his death and ask if they'd be interested in donating to the fund I put together in his name to fight substance abuse. As healthcare workers, they should be on board with that idea."

"That works." He liked the idea of going in soft, almost undercover. He didn't want to haul Craig or any of the other employees in for formal questioning until he had approval from his boss to reopen the case and until he had something more to go on. At the moment, he had a doc who'd been put in prison for fraudulently prescribing narcotics for his own personal benefit, as evidenced by the millions of dollars he'd hidden in overseas accounts. Craig Washington could easily claim ignorance of the scheme. Tarin needed something more to tie the pharmacist to the fraudulent scripts.

For a moment, he considered calling his brother Brady

who worked for the FBI. The Drug Enforcement Agency had jurisdiction over narcotics and other drug trafficking, but Brady or the other agents in the office may know more. Or provide a contact within the DEA who might be willing to share ideas about the scheme.

He finished his burger, deciding to make the call after his and Joy's visit to the pharmacy. He stood to take his dishes to the sink.

"Ready to go?" he asked.

Joy nodded. She was dressed much the way he was, in a bulky cable-knit sweater and jeans. The forest green of her sweater made her hazel eyes look green too.

And why did he care? He gave himself a mental shake and reached for his jacket. His phone rang, so he tossed the coat over the chair to answer his brother's call.

"What's up, Rhy?"

"We found a shell casing about twenty yards from the café."

"What caliber?"

"Nine-millimeter, which is the type of slug the Brookland PD believes they removed from your vic's door. It's not proof that's where the perp was standing when he took the shot, the shell casing could have been left at any time, by anyone. But there is a direct line of sight to the café, so it's reasonable to think the casing is from our guy. I thought you'd want to know."

"Thanks, Rhy." Tarin knew his brother was right, the casing alone didn't mean much. But the direct line of sight to the café was enough for him to believe the perp had made his first mistake. "Any fingerprints on the casing?"

"None, the shooter wore gloves. Not unusual in February. Sorry to cut this short, Tare, but I have to go. I'll be in touch later."

"That's fine." Tarin lowered the phone. He noticed Joy had listened to his side of the conversation, not that he blamed her. "They found a shell casing but nothing else yet."

"I guess something is better than nothing." She shrugged into her quilted jacket.

He pulled on his leather coat, too, hiding the PD sweatshirt from view, then led the way out to the garage. Once they were settled, he opened the garage door and backed out. As earlier, he took several twists and turns to get to Craig's Corner Pharmacy.

The place was smaller than he'd expected, the photos online had made it seem bigger. As he pulled in, he tried to understand how this place could possibly compete with the big guys.

"Ready?" He glanced at Joy.

"Yes. Let's go." She pushed open her door and slid out.

There were many shelves crammed into the small space, jam-packed with over-the-counter products. He was surprised to see there were three people in line, waiting to pick up their prescriptions.

Had another doc stepped in to take over Eli Lewis's fraudulent scheme? Or were these just returning customers obtaining their legitimate prescriptions?

Joy moved up behind the last person in line. He stayed close to her side, looking beyond the female tech working the sales register to the man wearing a white lab coat standing off to the side.

Craig Washington, he presumed. The pharmacist appeared to be about Tarin's age of thirty-five, give or take a year or so. After the clerk handed back the customer's credit card, Washington stepped forward to speak in a low voice to the woman before handing over her prescription bag.

"The pharmacist has to be the one to officially dispense narcotics," Joy whispered. "The techs and residents can hand off anything else, the pharmacist only has to ask if they have questions. But narcotics need to come from the pharmacist himself."

"Got it." He watched the woman who'd obviously just been handed some sort of controlled substance turn away, clutching the prescription bag close as she hurried past them.

The same routine took place with the next two people in line. Someone else came in to stand behind him, making Tarin doubt the wisdom of showing up in the middle of the day.

"Hi, Sue, I don't know if you remember me, I'm Ken's sister, Joy." Joy smiled at the pharmacy tech standing behind the counter.

"Oh, sure," Sue said with a nod. "Wow, it's been a long time."

"Five years," Joy admitted. She leaned forward to glance at the pharmacist. "Hi, Craig, it's nice to see you again."

"Joy." Craig did not smile back. "What brings you in?"

"Oh, well, I know this may not be a good time." She glanced guiltily at the man waiting in line behind them. "I'm sponsoring a fundraiser in Ken's memory, and I thought you might be interested in offering some support. I'm working with the Substance Abuse Prevention Advocacy."

The guy behind Tarin shifted impatiently. Craig's cheeks flushed red, but there was no evidence of anger in his tone. "Of course, but if you could come back another time, that would be best. Today has been very busy."

"Okay, that's fine." Joy didn't let his comment bother

her. "I know this issue must be important to you, Craig. I'm sure you see evidence of substance abuse in your role as a pharmacist."

"It is, yes." Craig's eyes narrowed. "But this isn't a good time. Please excuse me." Craig tilted his head making eye contact with the customer standing behind Tarin. "May I help you, sir?"

"Uh, yeah, but I forgot my wallet. I'll come back later." The customer abruptly turned and left the pharmacy, the bell jangling loudly as he did so.

"Oh, sorry about that." Joy pretended not to understand the guy's leaving was related to their discussion about substance abuse. "You're right, I'll come back another time. What days and times work best for you?"

"Here." Craig pulled out some cash and peeled off five twenty-dollar bills. "Take this as my contribution and Sue's too. Now if you don't mind, we really have a lot of work to do."

"Oh, this is wonderful, thanks!" Joy took the cash he'd set out. "I appreciate your support, Craig."

The pharmacist gave her a curt nod and turned away. He reached for the phone hanging on the wall and began dialing. Tarin wondered if the call was nothing more than an act or if the guy was calling someone to warn them about Joy's request.

"Bye, Sue," Joy said as she stepped back from the counter. Then she paused and asked, "Hey, who was the other tech that used to work here? I think he was a younger guy." She frowned. "I can't remember his name."

"Leon Webber, but he doesn't work here anymore. We have a new girl, Karen."

"That's right, Leon. Thanks, Sue." Joy flashed another

smile, pocketed the money, and turned away. Tarin followed her outside.

They didn't speak until they were back in his SUV. He started the engine, then looked at her. "What are you going to do with the money?"

"Donate it to the substance abuse program, of course." Then she sighed and tucked her hair behind her ear. "Craig is involved in the drug scheme, Tarin. After what we saw today, I'm certain of it."

"I have to admit, he came across as very suspicious." He rubbed his jaw. "And he clearly wanted nothing more than for us to get out of there."

"Did you notice how that customer left so abruptly?" Joy shook her head. "I don't understand why Craig would do something like this. He's a pharmacist, they make good money. And he owns his own business too. Why would he throw it all away on something like this?"

It was a good question. "I still need to dig into Washington's background, maybe I'll find a motive there. But in the meantime, he seems to be handing narcotics out like candy to trick-or-treaters."

Joy pursed her lips. "Maybe we're not being fair. I mean, there's a lot of people who legitimately need pain medication. This"—she waved a hand at the pharmacy in front of them—"is just a brief snapshot of what Craig does. He probably hands out other prescriptions too."

"I'm sure he does." Tarin didn't doubt the guy did whatever possible to come across as legitimate. "But I still think something fishy is going on."

"I do too." She sighed again, then lightly tapped his arm. "But as a wise detective once told me, we can't take action without proof."

Tarin couldn't help but smile. "Yeah, proof would be

helpful." He put the SUV in gear and backed out of his parking spot. The promised snow began to fall, big fat flakes hitting the windshield. Once he got home, he'd call Brady, then resume digging into Craig's personal life.

He took the long way back to his place, once again going out of his way to make sure he wasn't being followed. There was a traffic jam due to a disabled vehicle that caused them to sit for a full fifteen minutes without moving until traffic was rerouted around it.

As he drove down his street toward his house, a black car abruptly shot out from a side street right in front of him. He hit the brakes, his vehicle sliding a bit on the snow-covered road. He managed to avoid hitting the car that was sideways in front of him when the passenger window lowered, and a gun muzzle emerged.

"Gun!" he shouted, pulling Joy down as the windshield shattered beneath the force of a bullet. He abruptly hit the gas, sending his SUV directly lurching forward to strike the sedan in front of him. Someone cried out in pain. Tarin pulled his weapon and peered up over the dashboard.

Then the damaged sedan abruptly pulled forward, going up and over the curb, then turned and shot down the street, quickly disappearing from view.

CHAPTER SIX

Please, Lord, save us! The desperate prayer echoed in her mind as she bent forward, shards of glass from the damaged windshield covering her and the floor at her feet. Another black sedan, another gun.

When would it stop?

Never.

The grim realization hit her like a truckload of bricks. Whoever was doing this would never stop. Not until she was dead.

Useless tears leaked from the corners of her eyes, rolling down her cheeks. She'd never felt so helpless. Not even when Tarin had come to let her know Ken was dead. Her brother had been the only family she had left in the world, and his passing had been difficult to comprehend.

But this? This was much worse.

"Joy, are you okay?" Tarin's voice was urgent, and she risked lifting her head a few inches to look at him. "Don't worry, they're gone, but we can't stay here, we need to move."

"I-I'm fine." She didn't feel any pain. When she ran her

fingers through her hair, more glass rained down. "Is the car drivable?"

"Not exactly. We'll make it to my place, but that's about it." He put the car in gear and eased on the gas. The SUV rolled forward, tires crunching over debris on the road. "I need to call my brother and the Oakdale police."

The police hadn't helped so far. As soon as the unkind thought flashed through her brain, she shook it off. That wasn't fair. Tarin was a cop who had done everything possible to keep her safe. He'd placed himself in harm's way to accomplish that task.

This had been the fourth attack on her. Each one getting riskier. Or more desperate. On some strange level, she wondered if there were some sort of specific parameters, like a timeline the gunman had been given in which to accomplish his mission.

Or maybe that only happened in movies. Right now, she felt as if she was smack in the middle of a horror show. This couldn't be real.

Yet the shards of glass covering her clothes, hair, and the interior of the SUV were very real.

"Let's go, hurry." She belatedly realized Tarin had parked in his driveway. Moving sluggishly, she pushed open her door and slid out.

Tarin was at her side in an instant, covering her from the street as he hustled her up to the house.

"Pack your bag." He gave her a gentle push toward the hallway. She glanced at him, realizing he had his phone to his ear. "Rhy? I need backup ASAP. My SUV is damaged, and my house is not secure."

She didn't listen to the rest of the conversation. The urgency in Tarin's tone told her everything she needed to know. It didn't take her long to toss her things into the small suitcase. Picking up her laptop case, she carried it to the kitchen and stuffed the computer inside.

"Thanks, Rhy." Tarin disconnected from the call. "Okay, we're going out through the back. Rhy will pick us up a few blocks from here."

"Okay." She frowned when he took both her suitcase and laptop. "Aren't you packing a bag?"

"I have one." She belatedly noticed a duffel slung over his shoulder. He took her hand and led her to the back door. Without commenting further, he opened the door and stepped outside. "Stay close to me."

"Trust me, I will." She grabbed the back of his leather jacket, holding on tight. She couldn't navigate this nightmare that had erupted around her without Tarin.

He surprised her by cutting through his neighbors' yards, their footsteps leaving a path in the freshly fallen snow. She knew there wasn't a way to avoid it and kept glancing over her shoulder, deeply afraid the gunman would reappear.

When they reached the street, he walked along the tire tracks for a few blocks, then ducked down another home's driveway, then cut again through their backyard.

"What if they call the police to report trespassers?" she asked in a whisper.

"I am the police, remember?" He flashed a reassuring smile. "Don't worry, they won't. And even if they do, Rhy will be here soon enough."

One of the benefits of having a large family, she thought. There was never a lack of siblings to call for help in a pinch.

Her thoughts were rambling, her subconscious trying to keep her from thinking of the fourth near-death incident she'd suffered in twenty-four hours. Her foot slipped in the snow, but hanging on to Tarin kept her upright.

She glanced around nervously, on the brink of losing control. She needed to hold it together until they were safe.

Safe. A word she'd never take for granted ever again.

They reached the next street. Tarin walked down another set of tire tracks up to the corner. Then he finally stopped, taking a moment to look around.

"Is this our meeting spot?" It looked like every other neighborhood intersection, without a lot of trees or other foliage for cover. A window in the house to the right had a large red heart made of lights in honor of Valentine's Day. The holiday had passed, and she thought the red lights looked too much like blood.

Joy shivered, feeling vulnerable out in the open.

Headlights cut through the snow, the dark clouds making the hour seem much later than the two thirty in the afternoon displayed on her watch. Instinctively moving closer to Tarin, she watched the headlights with suspicion.

"It's Rhy," Tarin said reassuringly. He lifted a hand, and the vehicle slowed down. Tarin darted forward and opened the rear passenger door. "Get in."

She did so, relaxing in the warmth radiating from the vents. Tarin closed her door, then jogged around to stash her computer and suitcase in the back before getting in beside his brother.

She recognized Rhy from the scene of the café shooting. "Thank you for coming."

Rhy met her gaze in the rearview mirror. "You're welcome, it's no trouble at all." Then he shifted his gaze to Tarin. "You wanna tell me what's going on?"

"We need a safe place to stay for a while." Tarin sighed. "You should probably take us to the American Lodge."

"I thought you'd want to come to the homestead," Rhy said. "I put in that new security system two weeks ago."

Tarin hesitated and glanced at her. "I don't think that's a good idea. I don't want to put Alanna and Elly in danger."

"I would never put our family in danger, Tarin. The security system is designed to prevent intruders," Rhy said quietly. "Your choice. The good news is that we have a spare vehicle for you to use. Aiden has been deployed again to help in the Louisiana floods. You can use his truck in the interim."

Indecision creased Tarin's features. She didn't have anything to add to the conversation, other than to ask why they referred to the house as the homestead, so she held her tongue.

Yet the discussion nagged at her. Like Tarin, she wasn't keen on putting other innocent lives in danger too.

"Maybe we'll stay tonight," Tarin said. "We can head out tomorrow using Aiden's truck."

"Sounds like a plan." Rhy seemed satisfied. "Did you call the Oakdale PD?"

"Not yet." Tarin sighed. "My priority was to keep Joy safe, which meant calling you and getting her out of there. I don't understand how the shooter found us. I worked hard to make sure we weren't followed."

"Maybe they didn't have to follow you, they may have learned your identity from another source."

"How?" Tarin demanded. "There have been nonstop shooting attempts since last night! The only place my name would be is in police reports, and I seriously doubt a cop wants Joy dead."

The brothers were talking about her as if she wasn't there, and it was getting annoying. "I think you're both missing the point."

Tarin turned in his seat to look at her. "What do you mean?"

"I was taken off the bank audit today, and Benjamin was sent in my place. The real question is why this guy keeps coming after me? We thought it was related to the Trustworthy Bank audit irregularities, but this black sedan showed up right after we came back from Craig's Corner Pharmacy. And every pharmacy that stocks narcotics has security cameras inside and out."

Tarin stared at her for a long second. "You believe this is all related to your brother's death? To Craig and Dr. Lewis's drug scam? That this has all come to light since Lewis's arrest and conviction?"

"It's the only thing that makes sense." She frowned. "Well, except for the fact that they took a shot at me last night as I was trying to convince you to reopen Ken's case. How could they know I'd do that?"

"That's a good question," Rhy said in a grim tone. "Unless you've been under surveillance since the news of Lewis's arrest made headlines."

"That could be exactly what happened," Tarin agreed.

Joy felt sick to her stomach at the idea of some creep watching her for the past few days. Maybe for as long as a week. "They followed me to Paulie's, then also knew where I lived to show up there?"

Tarin nodded slowly. "And they knew you worked at the Trustworthy Bank and maybe even knew your routine was to eat lunch in the café each day. It makes sense, Joy, now that we know about the pharmacy."

She let out a heavy sigh. "So basically, these attempts reinforce my belief that Ken didn't kill himself. That he was, in fact, murdered because he knew too much."

"Yes." Tarin glanced at her. "Now all we need is proof."

She nodded, feeling numb from shock. She'd come to

Tarin out of desperation to clear her brother's name, but this?

Four attempts to shoot her in one day was more than she'd bargained for.

Unfortunately, stopping the investigation now wouldn't work either. It was too much like trying to put the genie back in the bottle.

No matter what she did or didn't do from this point forward, these gunmen would keep trying to silence her, fearing she already knew too much.

"The only way we can stop the danger is by uncovering the truth," she said in a weary tone.

Rhy and Tarin glanced at each other. Tarin turned and offered a reassuring smile. "Yes, I'm afraid you're right about that. But don't worry, we'll figure out who is behind this. And we'll keep you safe too."

"We?" She gestured with her hand between her and Tarin. "You mean the two of us?"

"No, I mean the entire Finnegan family." Tarin's eyes narrowed with determination. "I plan to use every resource I have to get to the bottom of this."

"We're happy to help, Tare," Rhy said.

She nodded, keeping silent about her concerns. It was bad enough Tarin was in danger because of her, but to drag in the rest of his family into this mess?

That was too high of a price to pay if things didn't work out the way they'd planned.

TARIN MENTALLY KICKED himself for not realizing the true motive behind these shooting attempts. He still believed Joy hadn't told anyone her intent to talk to him, but he hadn't anticipated that she may have been under surveillance for days, possibly weeks.

Going to Craig's Corner Pharmacy with Joy had been a big mistake. He'd honestly thought her audit was the reason for the attacks.

But apparently, Craig Washington was the guy responsible. He was still in business, no doubt working with some other shady doctors.

Or maybe he was even forging the prescriptions himself. Truthfully, Tarin wouldn't put anything past this guy. The way he'd all but pushed them out of the pharmacy indicated he had something to hide.

Not to mention the lack of enthusiasm upon seeing Joy after five years. Yeah, no question about it, the guy was hip deep in this scheme.

Rhy pulled into the driveway of the Finnegan homestead, interrupting his thoughts.

"Are you sure about this?" Joy asked hesitantly. "I really don't mind staying at a hotel."

"You'll be safe here," he assured her. It was not lost on him that he was doing the exact same thing Rhy had done a month earlier. Bringing a woman in jeopardy home to the family. If their father was alive, he would pitch a fit.

But their mother would have understood, welcoming the newcomer with open arms despite the danger. And when it came to his parents, Mom usually managed to get her way over their dad. The memory made him smile.

Rhy parked in the garage, the siblings knew it was his spot as head of the family, then closed the garage door behind them. Tarin jumped out of the car and went around to grab Joy's suitcase, laptop, and his duffel.

"Welcome to the Finnegan homestead," Rhy said as

they entered the kitchen. "You can use the last guest room, Joy. Tarin, you can use Aiden's room."

"That's fine. Follow me," he said to Joy. "I'll show you the guest room."

"How many bedrooms are there?" Joy gazed around the spacious home with admiration. "This place is huge."

"Nine kids and two parents, remember? Trust me, it did not feel huge when we were growing up and sharing rooms." Tarin headed toward the circular staircase leading to the second floor. "That's one of the reasons Rhy and I moved out as soon as we could afford it. But then had to move back in after our parents died. Still, there are lots of great memories here."

"It sounds amazing," Joy admitted.

"Sometimes, but not always," Tarin said dryly. "There are two hallway bathrooms upstairs, you can use either one, but this one is closer to your room and Devon's."

"Who is Devon?" Joy frowned. "I don't remember that name."

"She's Rhy's fiancée. Sorry, but it's a little like Grand Central Station around here." He crossed the threshold of the smallest room on the second level and set Joy's suitcase and laptop case on the bed. "Make yourself at home, I need to talk to Rhy about the security system, to learn exactly how it works."

"That's fine." She sank down onto the edge of the bed, looking around curiously. "This is very nice."

"Thanks." It was far better than a hotel, that was for sure. On one hand, he liked having Rhy close at hand if danger should come knocking. Yet he did not want Elly, Alanna, or Devon in harm's way either.

One night, he reminded himself as he headed back downstairs. Everyone should be safe enough for one night.

Rhy was on the phone when he entered the kitchen. "I'm on my way, give me maybe fifteen minutes because of the snow."

"Where are you going?" Tarin asked. "I need a quick refresher on the alarm system."

"I'm picking up Devon, the restaurant is closing early because of the storm." Rhy joined him at to the security display screen. After a few minutes, Tarin understood how it worked, and he liked the additional features of cameras stationed outside and around the property.

"It's great Rhy." He slapped his brother on the back. "You should have had it installed before you brought Devon here."

"I wish I had, but as it turned out, the house was never breached." Rhy shrugged. "I know I broke the rules, just like you're doing right now. It's not so easy to turn your back on a helpless woman in danger, is it?"

"No, it's not." A stab of guilt struck deep. "Sorry I gave you such a hard time about Devon."

"Don't worry about it. You were right to be concerned." Rhy's expression turned somber. "I'm worried about you too, Tarin. I was in your same situation just a few weeks ago. Thankfully, by God's grace, we all survived. Be careful, okay?"

"Always."

Rhy nodded. "Okay, you and Joy should be fine here. Elly is due home at any minute, but Alanna is working twelves and won't be off until seven thirty or eight. Devon prepared a meal before she went to work. Check the fridge, we're having roasted chicken, potatoes, and green beans for dinner."

"Sounds great, thanks again." Tarin waited for Rhy to leave before reengaging the security system. He thought about Rhy's comment and knew he was right. Rhy had put himself in danger several times when Devon had been on the receiving end of a crazed bomber.

The current situation with Joy wasn't much different. He hoped and prayed he could keep her safe long enough to get the man behind the gun arrested and tossed in jail.

He had two leads to work with—the pharmacy tech still employed at Craig's Corner Pharmacy, Sue, and the former tech, Leon Webber. The new girl, Karen, was a possibility, too, but he was more interested in why Leon Webber had moved on. Was the change a result of what was going on?

Would the techs even know what Craig was up to? He wasn't sure they'd be informed enough to understand the implications of dispensing so many narcotics.

Then again, the role did require schooling, so maybe he wasn't giving the techs enough credit. He only knew about the program because Elly had considered becoming a pharmacy tech. Of all the Finnegans, she was the least settled in her role. After one semester of attending the pharmacy tech program, though, Elly had switched to the emergency medical technician course instead.

The youngest Finnegan wanted to be a first responder like the rest of the family, even though he and Rhy had reassured Elly she could do whatever she wanted. Elly had dropped out of the police academy, had also decided against the nursing program after just two years, then switched her major again, before opting to attend the technical college to pursue a two-year associate's degree instead. Elly was scheduled to graduate as an EMT in May, and he, along with the other siblings, were holding their breath and praying that would happen. For her sake, not theirs. She needed to succeed.

As if on cue, the garage door opened, and the security

alarm let out a chirp. He silenced the alarm, then peered out the window to be sure Elly was the one who'd come home.

"Tarin! What are you doing here?" Elly asked. She tossed her backpack onto a chair and came over to hug him. "I hope you're staying for dinner. Devon made enough to feed an army."

"We are planning to stay, yes." He cleared his throat. "I have a guest with me, her name is Joy Munson."

Elly's eyed widened with interest. "A new girlfriend? It's about time."

"Hey, I don't mind being single," he protested. "And Joy is a friend that needs a safe place to stay, that's all."

"Yeah, that's what Rhy said about Devon a month ago." Elly flashed a cheeky grin. "See how that turned out? They're getting married next month."

"This isn't like that." He swallowed a sigh. Arguing with Elly was fruitless. She saw the world through her rose-colored glasses, which was one of the reasons he and his siblings were a little worried about her decision to become an EMT.

Personally, he worried Elly wasn't tough enough for the job, but he didn't want to come across as not supportive either, so he'd held his tongue. Elly was twenty-four, not fourteen. She'd have to figure things out for herself.

Bottom line, he and the rest of the Finnegan siblings would be there to support her no matter what.

"When can I meet her?" Elly asked as he reengaged the alarm. He was beginning to doubt the wisdom of having a security system when there were so many people coming and going.

He heard the fourth step from the bottom creak and knew Joy was coming downstairs. When he and Rhy had been younger, they'd sneaked out often enough to stay clear of the fourth step.

"Right now." He watched as Joy entered the room, stopping abruptly when she saw Elly standing beside him. "Joy, this is my sister Elly. Elly, this is Joy Munson. She's a CPA working for a large internal audit firm in Milwaukee." He'd purposefully added that part so that Elly could see the entire family didn't have to be EMTs, cops, firefighters, etc.

"Welcome to the Finnegan homestead, Joy." Elly greeted her with a wide smile.

"Thanks, it's nice to meet you." Joy frowned. "But why do you call it the Finnegan homestead? That's an old-fashioned term used in the eighteen hundreds when settlers first came to stake out their land for a home."

"You're absolutely right, it is an old-fashioned term. Our great-grandparents immigrated to Wisconsin from Ireland. I'm digging into our family tree using a variety of DNA sites. But the homestead is how our parents always referred to this place, the name just stuck." Elly turned to wink at Tarin. "I want to be Joy's partner if we play trivia. I bet she'll bury the rest of you with what she knows."

He smiled and shook his head. "Not sure about that, El. I usually win, remember?"

"Oh, you're good, Tarin, but Elly is right. I have a lot of useless information rattling around in my head." Joy flushed. "Comes from being a bit of a geek."

If she was a geek, which he highly doubted, she was the prettiest one around. And that was a dangerous thought, so he veered off that course right quick. "Sounds like Devon made dinner, so we have some time to work on the case."

Her expression turned grave. "Yes, we should do that. I know you're anxious to have me out of your hair."

"No, I'm determined to get the shooter behind bars," he corrected. "As soon as humanly possible.

"Shooter?" Elly echoed, her eyes widening with concern. "That doesn't sound good."

"It's not, but we're safe here." He gave his youngest sister a quick hug, then crossed over to Joy. "Come with me, Rhy has a small desk set up in the corner. We'll use that until he kicks us off."

Elly followed them into the living room, but then detoured to head upstairs. He settled in behind the computer, then turned to look up at Joy. "We'll look up Leon Webber first, see where he lives. I think he may know some information that could help us."

"You think he left the pharmacy because of the drugs?" The way Joy bent down to peer over his shoulder at the screen made his pulse kick up a few notches.

"It's possible." He forced himself to concentrate on the screen. "And what is Sue's last name? Do you remember?"

"Uh, let me think." She frowned. "Milburn? Milo? Something with an *M*. I didn't remember Leon until she reminded me."

Tarin did a quick criminal background check on Leon Webber. He didn't have a date of birth, but the ones that showed up on the screen were all older, in their fifties and above.

"Nothing so far," he muttered. "Let me try a regular search." He typed Leon Webber's name into a search engine, including the words pharmacy tech and Milwaukee and got a hit.

What bloomed on the screen was an obituary. Leon Webber, age twenty-eight, had died in a car crash four years ago. A year after Ken supposedly committed suicide.

An accident? Or murder?

CHAPTER SEVEN

Leon was dead. Just like her brother, Ken. Joy rested her hand on Tarin's shoulder as she read Leon's obituary on the computer screen. The obituary didn't say anything more about the cause of death to indicate that drugs or alcohol may have been involved, but it didn't matter. No way was this an accident.

"He was murdered too," she whispered.

"That is a distinct possibility," Tarin agreed somberly. He reached up to cover her hand with his. "I'll need to investigate the details of the case, get my hands on Leon's autopsy. But it does seem suspicious."

"It explains the series of attacks against me," she murmured. "Although this time, they're not bothering to make it look like an accident."

"The first attempt to shoot you down at Paulie's Pub may have been shrugged off as random," Tarin said. "But certainly not the next couple of attempts. I don't see how the gunman could know about the internal audit results, but if they did, they may have used that as a smokescreen, hoping that would be viewed as the reason for the attacks." He hesitated, then added, "That was our first theory."

She nodded slowly. "But here's what I don't understand. My being under surveillance wouldn't provide details about the audit. So how could they use that as a possible motive?"

Tarin abruptly stood and turned to face her. "Surveillance alone wouldn't give them that information. But if they tapped into your phone and/or your laptop? They'd know that and more."

The blood drained from her face. "Can they do that?"

"Not easily, unless they have some high-tech skills. But after four attempts, we need to make sure. Please give me your phone. We'll power it down and your computer too. I'd like to find a way to drop them off back at your place."

She pulled her phone from her pocket and handed it to him. "Take it. The computer too. It gives me the creeps to realize they may have been tracking or listening to me through either device."

"This could be overkill on my part." Tarin powered down her phone, then tucked it into his pocket. "But I'm not willing to take any chances."

"No argument here." She'd been exposed to enough danger to last a lifetime. "My computer is upstairs."

Tarin followed her up the grand staircase—the house was truly amazing—then he hovered in the doorway as she grabbed the laptop bag. She opened it on the bed and removed the computer. When she opened it, the screen came to life, so she quickly logged in just long enough to power it down.

Stepping forward, he took it from her. "I'll wait until Rhy and Devon get home before I go. I don't want to leave you and Elly alone."

"Okay." She frowned. "Although I'm not sure it's a smart idea to take the electronics to my place. What if the criminals involved in this are still watching it? Although, really, I can't imagine how many people they have on the payroll. It seems like a lot."

Tarin nodded thoughtfully. "You're right, it does seem as if the mastermind behind all this has a lot of resources at his or her disposal."

"And for what? A few million dollars?" She thought about the numbers she dealt with on a regular basis while performing audits. She dealt with hundreds of millions of dollars. The money found in Dr. Lewis's offshore accounts was pocket change in comparison. "Doesn't seem worth the risk if you ask me."

"I've seen far worse crimes for less," Tarin said with a shrug. "Nothing surprises me anymore."

It was difficult to understand the way some people had no regard or respect for human life, but then again, she spent her time with data and spreadsheets not people.

"Let's go back downstairs." Tarin stood back so she could precede him down to the main level. "I need to call my brother Brady."

She glanced over her shoulder at him. "He's the FBI agent, correct?"

"Good memory," he praised.

She flushed. "Sometimes, but not always." In truth, weird facts tended to stick in her brain more than people's names.

As they entered the kitchen, there was a chirping noise from the alarm system. Glancing outside, she saw a car pulling into the garage.

"Good, Rhy and Devon are home." Tarin slipped her phone into her computer bag with the laptop, then used his own phone to make a call. "Brady, it's Tarin. Give me a call when you have a minute, it's about fraudulent prescriptions that are being used to dispense narcotics."

"That's the DEA's role," she protested.

"Normally, yes. But they're all employed by the federal government, and I'm sure they've had to collaborate on cases, so I'm hoping Brady can point me in the right direction."

"We need all the help we can get." She turned as the door between the garage and house opened. A pretty woman with dark hair came in first, followed by Rhy.

"Hey, Tarin, great to see you." The brunette raised a brow at Joy. "Oh, you've brought a guest. Hi, I'm Devon Thompson."

"Joy Munson, nice to meet you." She stepped forward to shake Devon's hand.

"Rhy mentioned Tarin had brought someone to the homestead to keep her safe." Devon smiled. "I can relate. I was in a similar situation a month or so ago."

"The Finnegans obviously take their responsibilities seriously," Joy said.

"Especially Rhy and Tarin." Devon glanced back at her fiancé. "They held the family together after losing their parents ten years ago. And did a fabulous job, I might add."

"I couldn't agree more. I've only met Elly and Rhy so far, but everyone has been wonderful." Joy noticed Tarin went over to take care of the alarm.

"What's with this stuff?" Rhy gestured to the computer and phone.

"I need to borrow your car so I can put them at Joy's place." Tarin held his brother's gaze. "We don't know if they're bugged or not, but I'm not willing to take any chances."

Rhy whistled and tossed Tarin the keys. "Go ahead, and you may want to keep them plugged in and turned on at her place. Maybe you'll draw out the shooter."

"Yeah, I plan to put the Brookland police on notice. I'm going to request they make frequent patrols past her condo. Maybe catch the gunman trying to break inside."

"We'll need to be on alert here too," Rhy said.

The idea of the gunman finding her here made her blood run cold. "Maybe I should leave, go to a hotel."

"Not yet. Let's see if moving the phone and computer works first."

"You should take Joy with you," Rhy pointed out. "Make it look as if you're relocating her there."

Indecision crossed Tarin's features, but then he nodded. "Yeah, okay. You're right. Joy, are you up for this?"

No, she thought, but of course said, "Yes. Let's do it."

"Let the Brookland PD know you're heading over," Rhy suggested. "Maybe they'll put a squad in the area."

Tarin used his phone again, stepping away to make the call. Joy smiled at Devon, trying to hide her fear. "Congrats on your engagement."

"Thanks." Devon smiled at Rhy, her expression full of love. Rhy, too, grinned at his fiancée like a man besotted. "We're very happy, and I can't wait to become an official member of the Finnegan family."

A strange emotion hit Joy, a mixture of envy and longing. She could only imagine what it would be like to be a part of the family. Not that she was used to dealing with so many people, but still, there was no denying she felt safe here for the first time in what seemed like forever.

The Finnegans exuded confidence and skill. She did not doubt they would go to the mat for their siblings, and that included Devon now too.

She tried to think of something to say, but thankfully, Elly returned to the kitchen. "Hey, glad to have everyone together in one place. What time do you want to eat?" Elly's question seemed aimed at Rhy. "Looks like it will be the five of us tonight."

"Ah, whatever you decide is fine," Joy found her voice. "Tarin and I have an errand to run. It shouldn't take too long, but you don't need to wait."

"We'll wait," Rhy said firmly. "Tarin mentioned your condo isn't far. This little escapade should only take thirty or forty minutes, tops."

"We'll plan for dinner at six, then," Elly said. "Devon did most of the prep work already, so it won't take long."

The camaraderie between Devon and Elly was wonderful, and Joy tried not to feel like the outsider she was. Tarin returned and grabbed her quilted coat. "The Brookland PD will send a squad to your condo in about ten minutes, so we should hit the road now."

"Okay." She zipped her jacket, then reached for the computer bag. Tarin grabbed it first.

"I've got it. Let's go."

Leaving the warm Finnegan kitchen wasn't easy, but she reminded herself they'd be back soon. The snow was still falling, but lighter now, just a few wispy flakes. The temperature had dropped, though, so the seat warmer was amazing.

She needed to invest in seat warmers. As far as she was concerned, they were the greatest invention ever.

The closer they got to her condo, the tighter the knots grew in her stomach. It was only yesterday that someone had taken a shot at her outside her front door. And as Tarin pulled into the driveway, the bullet holes in her front door were a harsh reminder.

Tarin hesitated for a moment until a police squad arrived. The cop pulled over near her driveway, waiting for them to get inside. Tarin glanced at her and nodded. "Ready?"

"Yes." She pulled out her car keys, then pushed out of her side of the SUV. Tarin grabbed the computer case and followed her to the front door. She unlocked it and pushed it open.

Flipping on the lights, she quickly scanned the main living space, relieved it looked undisturbed. Tarin came in behind her, closing and locking the door.

"Set up your computer and your phone, I'm going to pull the car in the garage."

"Why?"

He shrugged. "When I leave, I want it to look as if I'm alone, and you're still here. It may be a stretch for anyone watching the place to believe I'd do that, but it can't hurt."

"I see." She did as he asked, listening as he opened the garage door, then drove the SUV inside. He spoke on the phone to someone, probably the officer sitting outside.

It didn't take long to power up her phone and computer, leaving them both on. The screen savers would make them go dark, but she was sure that some tracking equipment could still work. At least, her find my phone app did.

"Do you have any light timers?" Tarin asked.

She was about to say no when she remembered her Christmas tree. "I have one, I use it at Christmas."

"Perfect." Tarin smiled in satisfaction. "We'll set that timer up on a light in your bedroom. We'll keep the smaller kitchen light on too. Hopefully, that won't seem unusual."

"Okay." She led the way back out to the wall of shelving in her garage. She opened the box neatly labeled Christmas Decorations and removed the timer.

"You're very organized," Tarin said. "Our stuff is pretty much of a hodgepodge."

"Accountant, remember?" She refused to feel bad for being a bit obsessive about putting things in their proper place.

Once they had everything set, Tarin glanced at his watch. "Okay, time to go. I will need you to stay down in the vehicle, though, as we leave."

"I understand." Anything was better than being left here alone.

Tarin shut down the rest of the lights and went over to the garage door. She followed and slid into the passenger seat. Then she scooted way down, so that her head wasn't visible.

As Tarin drove back to the Finnegan homestead, she silently prayed this ruse would work. She wanted more than anything for the gunman to break into her condo and be caught by the Brookland police.

Please, Lord, stop this man's evil deeds before anyone else gets hurt!

THE SETUP at Joy's condo wasn't likely to yield fruit, but Tarin knew it was worth a try. He asked Joy to stay down the entire way back to the Finnegan homestead, just in case there was someone actually watching.

As he pulled into the driveway, he was glad to see that Rhy had shut all the drapes and blinds. The move was for safety reasons, but they valued their privacy too. He pulled into the garage, parking next to Rhy's SUV.

Rhy, Devon, and Elly were still in the kitchen when they came in. Rhy arched a brow. "How did it go?"

"Fine." His phone rang, and he was glad to see Brady's name on the screen. "Hey, Brady, do you have a few minutes?"

"Dinner in fifteen," Devon called after him.

He lifted a hand to indicate he understood. "I have a situation and need a DEA contact to get more information."

"The DEA doesn't like to share intel," Brady said. "But I think a fellow agent, Marc Callahan, has a DEA contact. I'll check with him."

Tarin frowned. "Marc Callahan of the possibly related to us Callahans?"

"One and the same," Brady drawled. "I mentioned the DNA connection to him, and he agreed that we share the same set of great-grandparents. I guess Elly's DNA match was spot-on."

"I just think it's weird that the Callahans are our cousins but we never knew about it," Tarin said. "I mean, why would that be some sort of big secret?"

"No clue, but I'm sure Elly and Maddy, Marc's sister, will get to the bottom of it. Oh, and get this, the Callahans have a set of twins in the family too."

"Wow. I mean, what are the odds of that?" Tarin asked. Personally, he wasn't sure what had possessed his parents to have such a large family, not that he didn't love each of his siblings. But the house had gotten far more chaotic when the twins had arrived. And then, of course, the oops baby, Elly, had come on the scene just three years later.

Much of those early days when he and Rhy had moved home were a blur in his memory. He'd been a street cop at the time, and learning the ropes while helping Rhy had taken all his energy. Yet he didn't regret moving home to help keep the youngest on track after losing their parents.

He'd do it again in a heartbeat.

"No clue," Brady said. "But give me some time, I'll try to get you a name tomorrow. What's this all about anyway?"

Tarin quickly filled his brother in on the four shooting attempts against Joy and their new theory that fraudulent scripts had motivated the attacks. "Dr. Eli Lewis was arrested and charged," he told Brady. "And when we visited Craig Washington's pharmacy, owned by Craig himself, he seemed annoyed to see Joy and obviously wanted us gone."

"That's very interesting, I'll see what I can dig up on Washington too."

"Thanks, bro." He glanced at his watch. "Is it okay if I call you tomorrow morning?"

"Sure, but you'll be at work, right?"

"No, I'm taking some personal time. I'm not leaving Joy here alone."

"You sound like Rhy," Brady complained.

He bit back a snarky response. Hard to argue when it was true. "Not the same thing, you have to admit, four attempts to kill her in twenty-four hours is highly unusual."

"Yeah, but Rhy's situation with Devon was also highly unusual. She had a bomber after her, and now you're protecting a woman from gunfire? Maybe the two of you are just cute victim magnets."

"Ha ha, very funny." Tarin glanced toward the kitchen. "Dinner is ready. I'll call you tomorrow."

"Okay." Brady ended the call.

Pocketing his phone, he returned to the kitchen. "Hey, Elly, did you know that one of the Callahans is an FBI Agent?"

"Marc Callahan is, yes." Elly smiled broadly. "Their family is similar to ours, but there are only six of them compared to our nine. Marc is the oldest and an FBI agent. Miles is the second oldest and is a detective, too, like you,

Tarin. Mitch is an arson investigator, Mike is a sheriff's deputy, like Kyleigh, Matt is a K-9 police officer, and his twin, Maddy, is the youngest, she works as an assistant district attorney."

"No lawyers here," Rhy said wryly.

"Yes, but she is a prosecutor, so she's still on the side of the good guys," Elly said, quick to defend her newfound relatives. "Maddy is trying to find out why we didn't know we were cousins, but so far, her mother hasn't had many answers."

"Probably some family scandal." Tarin grinned as he took a seat next to Joy. "Maybe you'll uncover some sort of family feud."

Elly looked distressed. "Wow, I hope not."

"Don't pay attention to Tare, he's teasing you." Rhy patted Elly on the back. "Nobody has feuds in this day and age."

"But they did back when our great-grandparents were around," Tarin felt compelled to point out. "They used dueling pistols and everything."

"That's enough, Tarin," Devon scolded. "Making up stories without knowing the truth is not helpful."

He shrugged. "Pays to keep an open mind."

"It also pays to think positive," Devon shot back.

She was right, so he let it go. Joy was unusually quiet, so he asked, "Are you okay?"

She nodded. "Just enjoying the moment."

Her words were like a punch to the gut. His family was like this day in and day out. No matter which of the siblings were home, the atmosphere was the same. Teasing, laughing, enjoying each other.

It was something he knew better than to take for granted.

"Here you go," Elly said, placing a large bowl of green beans on the table. Devon brought a tray of roasted chicken, and Rhy grabbed another bowl of tiny red roasted potatoes.

"This looks amazing," Joy said.

"Devon and Elly did most of the work," Rhy said. He folded his hands and glanced pointedly at Tarin. "Your turn to say grace."

Normally, Rhy did the honors as the head of the household, but Tarin simply nodded. "Dear Lord, we thank You for this warm meal You've provided. We ask that You continue to keep each one of us, those who are here and those who are not, in Your loving care. We also ask that You continue to keep Joy safe, in Jesus's name. Amen."

"Amen," the others echoed, including Joy.

The plates and bowls were passed around the table. The conversation turned to Rhy and Devon's wedding.

"It will be very small, nothing fancy," Devon told Joy. "But that's okay because I don't have any family to attend anyway, and the Finnegans are more than enough to fill a room."

"Does that mean I don't have to be the best man?" Tarin asked jokingly.

"You absolutely do," Devon responded. "And Elly will be a beautiful maid of honor."

"Sounds wonderful," Joy said.

Devon looked as if she'd say more, likely inviting Joy to attend, but Tarin gave her a warning glance. Joy wasn't here because they were dating. Quite the opposite. Rhy and Devon's wedding was four weeks away. By then the situation with Joy would be resolved, and they'd each go their separate ways.

The food was delicious as usual, and Tarin knew he and Rhy would need to do the dishes and clean up the table.

The Finnegan rule was that the cook did not have to clean up. And in his opinion, cleaning up was the easier end of the deal.

"I'll help you with those," Joy offered, jumping up to clear the table.

"No need, Rhy and I have it covered."

"Uh, actually, I have to make some calls, sorry." Rhy didn't look sorry, and Tarin suspected his brother was ditching him on purpose. "Joy, if you would take over for me, that would be great, thanks."

"Of course, it's the least I can do," Joy said firmly.

He shot Rhy a narrow glare but went back to filling the sink with hot soapy water. They rarely used the dishwasher; with so many kids, it was just easier to wash them by hand each day.

No surprise the rest of the family vanished from the kitchen, leaving him and Joy alone.

Really, the matchmaking was getting out of control. Just because Rhy had fallen in love with Devon didn't mean he was going to do the same thing with Joy.

"Idiots."

"Who, your family?" Joy asked.

He winced, not realizing he'd said that loud enough for her to hear. "They can be meddlesome."

"I think they're wonderful." Joy used a cloth to wipe off the table, then picked up a dish towel. "What did your FBI brother have to say?"

Tarin filled her in on his brief conversation with Brady. "I'm hoping the DEA knows more about these fraudulent scripts. It could be that pharmacist Craig Washington is already on their radar."

"I hope so." She glanced over at him. "It was nice of you to add me to the evening prayer."

"Your safety is important to me. To Rhy and the others too." He managed a reassuring smile. "And we believe in the power of prayer."

"I can tell it's not just lip service for you." She smiled sadly. "Ken and I were raised attending church, but since his death, I haven't been talking with God as much as I should be."

"It's never too late, Joy. God is always there, waiting for you to return."

"I know you're right about that. Thanks for showing me the way back, Tarin." She turned her attention to drying the dishes. When the job was finished, he took the dish towel from her and hung it on the oven handle to dry.

"Thanks for your help. Go relax for a while. I'm going to take a quick look around outside."

"Sure." She surprised him by giving him a quick kiss on his cheek. "Thanks again, for everything." She moved away before he could haul her into his arms for a proper kiss.

The way he wanted.

Not a date, remember? He pulled on his coat, then went outside to walk around the house. The dazzling white snow covering the tree branches and the ground was beautiful. He didn't see anything alarming, so he went back inside. Upon entering the living room, he frowned when he realized Joy wasn't there.

"She was tired and went to bed," Devon said, reading his thoughts. "I'm glad you brought her here to be safe."

"Me too." Tarin liked his sister-in-law to be. She fit into the family like one of their own. And Rhy certainly deserved to be happy. "Guess I'll head up too. Good night."

"Good night," Devon and Rhy said in unison.

Entering Aiden's room, Tarin was glad his youngest brother's National Guard made him a neat freak. He plugged in his phone next to the bed, then sighed. It was still rather early, but exhaustion nagged at him. He stripped down to his boxers and crawled into Aiden's bed, figuring he'd relax and unwind.

He must have fallen asleep because it seemed like just minutes later when his phone rang loudly beside him. He sat up, amazed to realize it was one o'clock in the morning. He picked up his phone, recognizing the first three numbers as belonging to the Brookland PD.

"Detective Finnegan."

"Detective? We thought you'd want to know your victim's condo is on fire."

"It's what?" Tarin wasn't sure he'd heard correctly.

"It's on fire, we have two fire trucks on scene. We caught it early, but you should know, we do not think this was an accident. We have reason to believe the blaze is the result of arson."

Arson. Why the sudden change in MO? A warning? Frustration in being tricked into thinking she was there?

Either way, it wasn't good.

CHAPTER EIGHT

"Joy, wake up." A hand shook her shoulder, drawing her from slumber. It took her a moment to remember where she was. "Joy?"

Tarin's voice grounded her yet also filled her with fear. He wouldn't wake her without a good reason. She sat upright, pushing her hair from her face. "What's wrong?"

"There's a fire at your condo." Even in the dim light, she could see compassion in his gaze. "I'm sorry, I feel terrible about this. I'm heading out there now and will let you know what I find."

"I'm coming with you." She was wearing her sleep shirt and shorts yet still felt a bit self-conscious with Tarin standing there. "Give me a minute to get dressed."

"It's better if you stay here."

"No. I don't have a phone, remember? I'll go crazy sitting here waiting without knowing what's going on." She waved him back so she could get up. "I'm going with you, Tarin. It's my home that's on fire."

She sensed his frustration as he turned away. "Fine, I'll wait."

The moment he'd closed the door, she shot out of bed and changed. She didn't take more than a minute to comb her fingers through her hair before joining him in the hallway. There was a light downstairs that partially illuminated the hallway, but the bedroom doors were all closed indicating everyone else was asleep.

She tiptoed after Tarin down the stairs. One of them squeaked, the sound seemingly loud in the silence.

"You'll need to stay in the car," Tarin said as he held her coat up for her to slip into.

"That's fine. Who called, the Brookland PD?"

"Yeah." Tarin grimaced as he shrugged into his own jacket. "The good news is that they caught it early thanks to the frequent patrols they did as a favor to me. The bad news is they suspect arson."

Arson? Dazed, she climbed into the passenger seat, trying to understand what this meant. This guy had taken shots at her four times, why the sudden switch to arson? It didn't make any sense.

Not that she was an expert in this kind of thing. As Tarin drove through Brookland toward her condo, she realized she'd rather work with spreadsheets and data than be thrust into life-and-death situations. The way Tarin and the rest of his family were.

It didn't take long for them to reach her condo, but they couldn't get close because the fire trucks were parked in front of the place.

Tarin frowned. "I changed my mind, I don't want you to wait in the car. It's too far away from the scene. You'll have to come with me."

"Thank you." She gladly pushed open her door to join him in the chilly February night. "I won't get in the way."

"That's not what I'm worried about." Tarin took her

hand. "I need you to be safe, Joy. That's the most important thing."

"I'm safe with you, Tarin." And she felt safe with the other Finnegans too. As they approached the fire trucks, she searched for signs of the fire. "I don't see any flames."

"I'm sure they have the fire under control." Tarin stepped up to the closest firefighter. "I'm Detective Finnegan. This condo belongs to a woman who is a victim of several shooting attempts."

"Oh yeah, I heard about that." The fireman turned to look at her curiously. "This your vic?"

"Yes, I'm Joy Munson, and that's my condo." She couldn't smile, the blackened doorway of her home was horrifying to see, even from here. "I—do you have any idea what happened?"

The firefighter shrugged. "Not yet, the scene is too hot. We called the arson investigator, Mitch Callahan, to come take a look."

The name reminded her of Elly's DNA work. Not that the family connection was important in the face of the fire.

"Where is Officer Patrick Cohen? He's the one who called me." Tarin glanced around the busy scene.

"Near the two squads." The firefighter gestured toward them. "You'll need to stay back from the property. The fire is out, but we haven't officially cleared the scene."

"My brother Colin is a firefighter, so I understand how it works." Tarin gave the guy a nod. "Thanks for the quick work here."

"It's part of the job. I'm just sorry it had to happen at all." The firefighter shot her a sympathetic look. "On a positive note, there are no casualties. The neighbors all escaped without a problem."

Joy was ashamed to realize she hadn't asked about her

neighbors. When Tarin mentioned they'd gotten to the fire early, she'd assumed they were fine. Not something she should ever assume, especially with this evil man on the loose. "I'm relieved to hear that."

"Me too," Tarin agreed. "Let's see what Officer Cohen has to say."

She followed Tarin past the fire trucks and across the street to where the two Brookland PD squads were parked. "Officer Cohen?"

"You must be Detective Finnegan." A man roughly her age stepped over to shake Tarin's hand. "I'm sorry we didn't catch this guy for you."

Tarin nodded. "He certainly changed his approach, that's for sure. Can you tell me what happened?"

"We were doing our usual rounds through the neighborhood, focusing on this condo as requested, when we saw a flickering light inside." Cohen's expression was grim. "I could tell something was on fire, so I called it in. I couldn't search for the perp as I needed to evacuate the residents from the surrounding homes."

"Understandable, I appreciate your efforts. You didn't see any suspicious vehicles or pedestrians lurking nearby?" Tarin asked.

"No, sorry. But the weird thing was that I could see the fire was localized to the bedroom, specifically the bed itself, not the kitchen, which is where most fires start. That alone made us believe the source to be arson."

A shiver of unease skittered down her spine. Why had this guy burned her bed? That seemed incredibly odd to her. As if it was some sort of personal message or something. Which was strange because up until now, the shootings had been done from a distance.

Although maybe her not being in the condo was what

had fueled the desire to burn her bed. An impending sense of doom hit hard. Joy couldn't help but wonder if the action had been designed to tell her she'd never be able to escape.

Instinctively, she moved closer to Tarin. He squeezed her hand reassuringly. "Thanks to your quick work, the fire was put out quickly."

"Yes, but there will be a lot of water damage," Officer Cohen warned. "The firefighters doused everything inside the place to prevent the fire from spreading."

"I can deal with water damage," she said. It wouldn't be easy, as the repairs would take time, but better to have severe water damage to her condo than suffering loss of life.

"I guess it's too late to search for footprints now." Tarin scanned the area. "Looks like the firefighters swarmed the place."

"They did," Officer Cohen agreed. "We'll canvass the neighbors in the morning, but everyone I evacuated had been asleep when the fire started." The cop shrugged. "Sorry to say, but I don't think we'll learn much. Other than it looks like he accessed the condo through one of the bedroom windows. The firefighters had to break in the front door to fight the fire. The oxygen coming in through the broken window fueled the blaze."

Her bedroom window. It seemed like this guy would do anything to get to her. A wave of frustration threatened to overwhelm her. It seemed that no matter how hard they tried to track the evidence, this evil man eluded them. Gazing at her waterlogged and partially burned house, she found it hard to believe all this had been done because of drugs and money.

"Thanks, Cohen. Appreciate your efforts." Tarin turned away from the squads. Still holding her hand, he drew her back to where they left Rhy's SUV. "I'm sorry my plan was such a colossal failure."

"It wasn't a failure, the shooter obviously came to look for me." She shivered, realizing what might have happened if she'd been home. "No one could have anticipated that he'd set the place on fire."

"I should have realized he'd be angry about being duped." The hard edge of self-recrimination underscored Tarin's tone. "He clearly took his anger out on you, personally, starting the fire in your bedroom."

She glanced back at the condo. "I think it's strange that he broke into my bedroom. If he'd looked inside, he'd have known I wasn't there, despite my phone and computer being set up to make it seem like I was."

Tarin grimaced. "When he realized it was a trap, he got angry, broke in, set the fire, then booked out of there."

"I still don't see the point in doing all of that," she protested. "He could have just moved on, searching for a new way to find me."

Tarin abruptly stopped, pulling her close to his side. "Maybe he's out there right now."

"Really?" Her voice came out in a high squeak. The fire trucks and police vehicles put out plenty of light, but darkness lingered behind the neighborhood homes. "Why?"

"He's feeling desperate," Tarin said grimly. He pulled his weapon and held it ready as he cautiously approached the vehicle. "Stay close. I need to check out the SUV."

She tightened her grip on his hand, glancing around nervously. She wanted to believe no one was brazen enough to come after her this close to dozens of first responders, but Tarin's concern was infectious. If he was worried, she was doubly worried.

Tarin let go of her hand to grab his phone. She

latched onto the edge of his coat as he shined his light inside the SUV, making sure it wasn't occupied. When he finished, he opened the passenger door for her. "Get in and keep the doors locked. I need to check the under carriage."

"For what?" She slid into the seat as requested.

"Tracking device." He shut the door, waited until she triggered the lock, then went down onto the ground. She couldn't see exactly what he was doing, but as the seconds ticked by, she couldn't control her shivering.

After what seemed like forever, Tarin appeared at the driver's side window. He used his key fob to unlock the door, then slid in behind the wheel. "Find anything?"

"No, thankfully." He still looked somber as he started the car. "But I'm not heading straight home either. I don't want to lead this guy to the homestead."

She frowned. "Where will we go?"

"The American Lodge motel." He started the car and shifted into gear. "It's clean and will do in a pinch."

"Your family will worry."

"I'll send Rhy a text, he'll understand." Tarin drove out of the subdivision. "This is the way it has to be."

She nodded, trusting Tarin's instincts. If he was worried the shooter turned arsonist might follow them, then it was better to avoid his family.

Even though she wasn't quite ready to leave them behind. She'd enjoyed her brief time with Tarin's family, a little too much for her own peace of mind.

HE'D BEEN a complete idiot to rush out to the crime scene. Tarin inwardly railed at himself for making such a rookie mistake. Sure, he'd been sound asleep and thinking only of the possibility of getting this guy.

But he should have considered the perp had done this specifically to draw them out of hiding. How could he have been so foolish?

His fault for thinking like a guy who cared about a woman rather than a cop working with a victim. He sternly lectured himself against allowing such a thing to happen again. Joy was not his girlfriend, and he needed to stay focused on working her case.

Rather than taking her home and introducing her to some of his siblings.

He ground his teeth together so hard his jaw hurt. Keeping an eye on the rearview mirror revealed there was no one behind him, but he wasn't going to assume anything.

No, at this point, he'd plan for every single possibility, no matter how unbelievable.

Starting with spending the rest of tonight and subsequent nights at the American Lodge. Which was what he should have done from the very start of this mess.

He told himself it wasn't too late to get back on track. In fact, he may be able to use the American Lodge as the next trap. It was a trick Rhy had done a month ago when Devon was in danger.

Rhy's plan hadn't worked then, just like his recent plan to draw the shooter to Joy's condo had backfired. He'd need to think it through a little more, maybe get some help from Brady too.

The danger surrounding Joy had gone on long enough. It was well past time to catch this guy.

"Are you upset with me?"

Joy's comment struck a nerve. "No, of course not." He tried to lighten his tone since the person he was most annoyed with was himself. "I just think the American Lodge is better in the long run."

"I agree. Elly and Devon don't deserve to be in danger because of me."

"You deserve to be safe too, Joy." Yet he couldn't deny his family had to come first. "We'll figure out how to get a lead on this guy. I'll talk to Brady and the DEA tomorrow. I'm sure I can convince them to dig into Craig's Corner."

"I hope so." She didn't sound convinced, and he couldn't blame her. If only he'd done a better job of investigating her brother's death five years ago, they wouldn't be in this situation today.

Unfortunately, he couldn't go back and change the past. But he could make a better effort to minimize his mistakes going forward.

He absolutely needed to avoid messing up the investigation any more than he had already.

There was a single light on in the lobby of the American Lodge motel. Tarin parked in front of the doors, then slid out. He opened Joy's door, refusing to let her out of his sight.

"You need a room?" The clerk eyed him and Joy warily.

"I'm Detective Tarin Finnegan, you may remember my brother Rhy who came to visit last month." He smiled at the clerk, trying to reassure the kid. "I'm sure Gary Campbell is asleep, but we could use a set of connecting rooms if you have them available."

"Oh yeah, Finnegan. I remember." The kid brightened. "Gary's at home, but I can send him an email to let him know you're staying here."

"That would be great." Gary was a retired firefighter and was well known in the community as a great host to cops and firefighters alike. "Thanks."

"I'll give you the cop rate," the kid said. "I'm sure Gary won't mind."

A few minutes later, he and Joy had the keys to their respective rooms. Tarin escorted her back outside, glancing around curiously. There were five other cars in the parking lot, indicating the motel wasn't full. During the summer and fall, rooms here were harder to get.

Their connecting rooms were on the first floor at the opposite end from the lobby. Tarin parked his brother's SUV around the corner, out of view.

He waited for Joy to unlock her door, then followed her inside. "I know it's nothing fancy, but Gary runs a clean place."

"It's fine." She stood for a moment in the center of the room. "I wish I'd been able to pack a few things, though."

"We'll take care of that tomorrow, Rhy will probably want to swap out his SUV anyway, so I'll have him bring our bags." Tarin went over to unlock the connecting door. "I need you to leave this open for me, okay? I won't intrude on your privacy, but if something happens, I need to be able to get to you quickly."

"Sure." She dropped onto the edge of the bed. "I'll be fine."

He felt bad for putting her through all of this, but she was the one who'd insisted on coming along. He went over to rest his hand on her back. "I'll protect you, Joy."

"I know you will." She stared down at her hands for a moment, then surprised him by looking up and asking, "Will you say a prayer for me?"

"Of course." He knelt on the carpet and took her hands in his. "Dear Lord, we thank You for keeping the residents around Joy's condo safe in Your care. We ask that You continue to shield us from those who seek to harm Joy. Amen."

"Amen," she whispered.

"You're going to get through this," he said, his heart aching for her. His stern lecture about keeping her at arm's length was becoming a distant memory. "God will watch over us, and I will do everything possible to protect you."

She didn't say anything for a long moment. "It just seems so inevitable that he'll find and kill me."

He understood her feelings of helplessness, he'd experienced the same thing when Caroline had been killed. "I know it's not easy, but you must know that with God anything is possible."

She tried to smile. "That does help."

He rose and took a seat beside her on the bed. "I'm the one battling guilt over this. I dropped the ball five years ago. I know I told you that I'd recently lost my partner, Caroline, two weeks before being assigned to your brother's case." He sighed. "I failed to mention Caroline was more than just my partner, we'd started seeing each other on a personal level. I was devastated when she was killed, and it was even worse because I didn't have a chance to tell my family about our relationship."

"Did you think they wouldn't approve?"

"Not exactly, although I can't deny I expected some grief from Rhy and Kyleigh. As cops, they would be quick to point out that cops who are partnered together aren't supposed to get emotionally involved."

"That must have been so difficult for you, grieving over her loss without your family's full understanding and support."

She was right about that. "Yes, but there was no point in

telling them the truth after the fact. And maybe I didn't want to admit that her death may have been my fault."

"Your fault?" Joy echoed in shock. "Why on earth would you say that?"

"I was cleared of any wrongdoing by the department," he hastened to explain. "But I still felt guilty. I told her to take the back of a building where a homicide suspect was hiding. I took the front. Turned out, the guy bolted out back, shooting his way as he exited the building."

"So, not your fault at all."

"I could have taken the back. If I had considered this guy's penchant for running, I would have realized he'd go that way." It was a decision that would haunt him for a long time.

"Because you can read minds?" Joy scoffed. "I don't think so."

That was the exact same thing Kyleigh had said to him after the incident. The memory made him smile. "No, I can't read minds, and playing Monday morning quarterback is easy. It's taken me some time to admit that this was part of God's plan. I don't why, but that's not for me to know. God asks us to place our trust in Him, so I need to accept it and move on."

"That sounds easier said than done."

"It is. We're human, and we make mistakes." Like sitting here telling Joy his deepest secrets. "But if we ask God for support and guidance, He will be there for us."

She nodded thoughtfully. "I believe that too, Tarin. Obviously, it's easier to turn to Him when we're in danger, but I know He is there through good times and bad." A smile tugged at the corner of her mouth. "I love the way your family prays before meals."

"Long-standing habit, drilled into us by our parents.

Rhy made a point of continuing the tradition after they passed away, and I'm glad we did. Our faith bonded the family together during that difficult time."

"Makes me wish I'd have turned to God after Ken's death."

"He knows your heart, Joy." He wrapped his arm around her shoulders, giving her a quick hug. "That's what matters."

"I hope so." She rested her head on his shoulder.

They sat together for a long moment. Tarin knew he needed to get into his own room, but he was hesitant to leave. Finally, he released her and eased away. "I need to go. Don't be startled when I open my side of the connecting doors."

"I won't." She continued sitting on the bed as if she didn't have the energy to move. Her fragile expression tugged at his heart, but he forced himself to leave.

After slipping from her room, he closed the door behind him and looked around the parking lot again. He pulled out his phone and took pictures of each license plate on the five vehicles. Then he unlocked his room and went inside.

He took a moment to unlock and open the connecting door before examining each license plate number more closely. Maybe he was being paranoid, but he crossed over to the motel phone and made a call to the precinct. "This is Detective Finnegan, I'd like to speak with Sargent Sullivan."

"Just a moment." He was put through to the sergeants desk a second later.

"Sullivan."

"Sarge, it's Detective Finnegan. I need you to run a few plates for me."

"At two o'clock in the morning?" Sullivan sounded skeptical. "Why?"

Tarin didn't want to go into detail, especially since his lieutenant didn't know he'd reopened the Ken Munson case. "These five cars have been identified as being suspicious. All I need are the names and addresses of the owners."

Sullivan sighed heavily. The sound of fingers hitting a keyboard clacked in the background. "Give them to me."

Tarin did so, one license plate at a time. When Sullivan had the name and address of the registered owner, he jotted them down on the motel notepad. Not one of the names sounded familiar, and every single address was from locations outside the Milwaukee area, as would be expected for a motel.

"Anything ring a bell?" Sullivan asked when they'd finished.

"No, but I might dig into them in more detail. Thanks for your help, Sarge."

"Yeah, why don't you get some sleep, Finnegan? Tomorrow is another day."

"Copy that, Sarge. Good night." He hung up the phone and stared down at the names and addresses he'd been given.

Yeah, he was paranoid all right. There was no possible way that any of Craig Washington's hired thugs could know that he'd brought Joy to the American Lodge.

Joy was safe here.

Now, he just needed to figure out a way to keep her that way.

CHAPTER NINE

The murmur of a deep voice from Tarin's room roused her curiosity. Joy hovered in the doorway of their connecting rooms, but now he was quiet. She poked her head inside his room. "Is there a problem?"

"What?" Tarin glanced up. "No."

"I heard you talking to a sarge, I assume short for sergeant." She came into the room and took a seat at the small table there. "Did you learn anything new about the shootings or the fire?"

"Afraid not." He hesitated, then added, "I had the night sergeant run all the plate numbers of the cars outside to provide me with names and addresses of the guests staying here."

"You did?" She stared at him in shock. "Why? They were here before we were."

"I know. I just—needed to be sure." He looked chagrined. "After everything that has happened, I figured it was better to be hypervigilant."

Guilt was an emotion she understood all too well. She'd felt responsible for Ken's death, even though she'd never believed he'd taken his own life. The mere possibility was enough to make her wonder what she'd missed.

Now, she could see grooves of guilt carved in Tarin's face. "None of this is your fault. Not the fire at my condo or any of the four shooting incidents. You've protected me every step of the way."

He shrugged, not looking as if he agreed. "I need to do better. Starting now. You should get some sleep, Joy. We both need to rest up. Tomorrow, I hope to get in touch with the DEA through my brother's connections within the FBI. I'm sure it will be another long day."

"Okay." She was glad they had connecting rooms, or she'd never sleep a wink. Just being close to Tarin gave her a sense of security. And if he was right about the FBI and the DEA, tomorrow would be a long day. She rose, fighting the urge to go over to kiss him. "Good night, Tarin."

"Good night." He didn't stand to walk her to the door, which was what he'd normally do. She crossed the threshold of the connecting doorway, stepping into her room. She shut the door partway behind her, leaving it open about a foot, then went into the bathroom to wash up.

Yeah, kissing him was a bad idea. Especially after hearing about how much he'd loved Caroline. Not that he'd said the words but she could tell his former partner was important to him, both professionally and personally.

Now she understood why a guy as handsome and nice as Tarin didn't have a woman in his life. He'd shut himself off after losing the one he'd loved.

And that was that. She stared at her reflection for a moment, then turned away. Being with Tarin like this wasn't real. Her life was routine and boring. This running from bad guys with guns was something from a movie.

Okay, maybe the running from guns part was real but

not this intimate connection she felt with Tarin. The sooner she accepted that, the better.

Sleep would be impossible, but she did her best to rest anyway. Normally, she didn't have trouble sleeping, but everything about these past two days had been far outside her area of expertise.

Remembering Tarin's prayer, she repeated it in her mind, her muscles slowly relaxing as she did so. Then she must have fallen asleep because the next thing she knew sunlight was stinging her eyes.

Blinking, she sat up, realizing she'd forgotten to close the blinds. Maybe because she'd slept in her clothes, unwilling to strip down with Tarin right next door. Not that she didn't trust him, because she did. He'd treated her with the utmost respect every step of the way.

She climbed from the bed and closed the drapes halfway. Glancing at the clock, it was nearly eight in the morning. She'd slept later than she'd intended.

After washing up in the bathroom, she went over to listen at the connecting doorway. "Tarin?" she called softly. "Are you awake?"

"Yes, I'm up. Would you like some coffee?"

"Please." She went into his room. "I'm sorry I slept so late."

"You didn't," he assured her. "I'm glad you were able to get some rest. I managed to get a few hours too, but we should head out to grab breakfast soon. I'd like to be ready once Brady calls with his DEA contact."

"Of course." She sipped her coffee, looking at him over the rim. "Look on the bright side, we don't have anything to pack."

"Good point." He grinned, and she thought he looked better today. Maybe not as stressed as he'd been last night.

Or rather, a few hours ago. "We're going to meet Rhy at the family restaurant about a mile from here in an hour. He's going to grab his SUV and leave us with Aiden's truck."

"Sounds reasonable. Rhy wasn't upset with you, was he?"

"No, why would he be?" Tarin looked confused. "He knew I needed the SUV."

More proof of the camaraderie between the Finnegan siblings. "I wasn't sure how he'd react knowing you took his SUV but didn't return home."

"He's fine." Tarin brushed off her concern. "We need to stop in the office to arrange to keep these rooms for another day."

"Okay." She hid her disappointment by drinking more coffee. The American Lodge was fine, but she couldn't deny that staying at the Finnegan homestead had been much better. Not an option, of course, since Tarin was determined to keep his family safe.

She couldn't blame him. If Ken was still alive, she'd do everything in her power to keep him safe too.

And for the first time, she doubted the wisdom of coming to Tarin for help in reopening Ken's case. He was gone, and her poking around to uncover the truth had only put her in the crosshairs of some trigger-happy nutjob.

It was too late to go back and do things differently now.

Twenty minutes later, they were on the road heading to the restaurant. Tarin took several detours, the way he had last night, before pulling into the parking lot and shutting down the engine.

Inside the restaurant, the tantalizing scent of coffee and bacon greeted them. Tarin drew her toward a booth in the back corner. "This okay?"

"Fine." It was far from the doorway but closer to the

restrooms, so she didn't mind. When Tarin sat facing the door, she understood he would be watching for his brother Rhy.

Their server brought coffee, then took their orders. Tarin had his phone on the table beside him and kept glancing at it every ten seconds, anticipating Brady's call.

When the phone buzzed, he jumped on it. "Hey, Rhy. Are you joining us for breakfast?" A pause, then, "Okay, I'll be out in a sec." He set the phone back down and slid out of the booth. "Rhy asked Elly to pack your stuff, so your suitcase and my duffel are in Aiden's truck."

"That was thoughtful of him."

He grinned. "Rhy likes to delegate. I guess that's what makes him a good captain. This won't take long. If Brady calls, keep him on the line until I get back."

"Will do."

Tarin's phone didn't ring, even after he returned to the table. Their breakfast arrived, and this time she knew what to expect. Yet she was surprised when Tarin reached across the table to take her hand. She secretly savored the warmth of his fingers cradling hers. "Lord, we thank You for this food and ask You to continue keeping us safe in Your care. Guide us as we seek justice. Amen."

"Amen." She reluctantly released him. "I hope you're right about seeking justice. I can't help thinking I should have left Ken's case alone."

Tarin frowned. "I know you've been through a lot, but if Craig did have your brother killed, he needs to go to jail. Besides, he's still breaking the law. Who knows how many other people he's hurt with this scheme he and Eli Lewis cooked up? Drug addiction is a serious problem, and getting rid of people responsible for that is the right thing to do."

"You're right." She sighed and took a bite of her eggs. It

was selfish to only think about herself. "I want Craig and whoever else is involved to be held accountable for their crimes."

"They will be." They ate in silence for a few minutes. Tarin glanced frequently at his phone, but there was still nothing from Brady.

She hoped that didn't mean bad news. It occurred to her she needed to call her insurance company about the fire at her condo, but she didn't have a phone. "Any chance we can stop to pick up a new phone? Not using the same number," she hastily reassured him. "Just something to use in the interim."

"Of course, I should have thought of it sooner." He grimaced. "Both your phone and your computer are water damaged, I'm sure."

"Yeah." She tried not to feel overwhelmed at everything she'd need to replace at her condo. It seemed frivolous to worry about her clothes, electronics, and furniture when there had been four attempts to shoot her.

She was alive, and that was all that mattered. Closing her eyes, she silently thanked God for keeping her and Tarin safe.

His phone rang, and he quickly picked it up. "Hey, Dave. Sorry, I should have reached out sooner. Did the lieutenant let you know I'm taking a few days off?"

She couldn't hear the other side of the conversation, but based on Tarin's expression, his partner wasn't very happy.

"Yeah, I know this puts you in a bind, but it can't be helped. Do you best on our open cases, and I'll be in touch as soon as I wrap things up here, okay?"

Another pause, then Tarin disconnected from the call and set the phone back on the table.

"Your partner?" she asked.

"It's fine, nothing to worry about." Tarin brushed aside her concern. "Dave won't miss me that much, he has open cases to work."

"What about new cases?" She wasn't sure how things worked. "Will they assign him to someone else?"

"They might, depending on the case." He met her gaze. "You don't need to worry about me or Dave. You're the one in danger."

She nodded and let it go. If Tarin wasn't going to worry, she wouldn't either.

When they finished eating, Tarin insisted on paying the bill. The way he scowled at his phone would have been funny if her situation wasn't so serious.

"Maybe you should call Brady," she suggested as they headed out to Aiden's truck.

"I will." He was still scowling as he held her door for her. "Brady should have something for me by now."

Once they were seated, Tarin made the call. She was glad he had the call go through the dashboard system so she could hear too.

"Hey, Tarin, sorry for the delay." Brady sounded rushed. "I spoke with Marc Callahan first thing, and have made contact with Doug Bridges, the DEA agent Callahan has worked with in the past."

"Doug Bridges?" Tarin repeated as if committing the name to memory. "Shoot me his contact information in a text."

"I will, although I'm waiting for him to call me back. I wanted to give Bridges a heads-up in case he wasn't exactly the right guy to go to."

"I need help with this case ASAP," Tarin said curtly. "Last night the perp started a fire in Joy's condo."

"A fire?" Brady sounded shocked. "Why would he

suddenly change his MO after shooting at her so many times?"

"I have no idea, which is why I need help unraveling this case. My gut is telling me Craig Washington is behind this, but I don't have proof that he's doing anything illegal. Other than sketchy customers coming in to fill narcotic prescriptions."

"I hear you, Tare. I have another call coming in, let me grab this. If it's Doug Bridges, I'll call you back."

"Thanks." Tarin hit the end button to disconnect from the call. He pulled out of the restaurant parking lot, merging into traffic.

"Where are we going?"

"The FBI offices, I think we need to speak with Brady and this Doug Bridges agent in person."

Before she could say anything, Tarin's phone rang again. He put the call on speaker. "Finnegan."

"Tarin, I have Agent Bridges on the line too," Brady said. "I was explaining about your case, and he's very interested in anything connected with Dr. Eli Lewis."

"Good, where can we meet you?" Tarin asked.

"We can meet at the federal building," a deep male voice said. "Your brother Brady has a conference room he'll let us use."

"We'll be there in twenty," Tarin said.

"See you then."

She glanced at Tarin after he disconnected from the call. "Do you think this will work? That the DEA and the FBI can help us figure out what's going on?"

"It has to," Tarin said grimly.

Swallowing hard, she tried to relax. Surely having additional support from the feds was a good thing. Obviously, she couldn't hide from the gunman forever, not even with Tarin's help.

Yet she couldn't help but wonder if Tarin planned to hand her over to this new DEA agent. On one hand, she couldn't blame him. He had a life and a job of his own to do.

But on the other hand? She really wasn't ready to let Tarin go.

AFTER WHAT FELT like swimming in the dark without a life jacket, he was glad to have the opportunity to sit with Bridges and his brother to create a plan. He kept a wary eye on the rearview mirror, watching for a possible tail, but if the gunman was following them, he'd be disappointed to learn their destination was none other than the FBI office building.

Rush-hour traffic was its usual mess after a snowstorm. Normally, he was a patient driver, but today he was irritated with every vehicle that got in his way. He was anxious to reach the federal building, if nothing more than to have some peace of mind in knowing Joy would be safe there.

Too bad they couldn't live there, he thought wryly. He glanced at Joy, who seemed lost in her own thoughts.

"Hey, this is going to work out great." He infused his tone with confidence. "I have a feeling Doug Bridges will know all about Craig Washington's little side business. The information you have related to your brother's death and what we know of Leon's passing may be just what they need to close him down."

"I hope so," she agreed. "But it does make me wonder why they haven't closed him down already. I mean, what are they waiting for?"

Good question. "I'm not sure, but we'll know more when we meet with Doug and Brady." He had the utmost faith in his brother. "Maybe they're trying to figure out who else is involved in the scheme."

"Maybe." He could tell she was less than enthusiastic about this side trip, and he didn't understand why.

"Trust me, okay?" He took her hand in his.

"I do trust you, Tarin." She offered a wan smile. "I'm sure the feds will come up with a good plan."

They'd better, he silently agreed.

Checking the rearview mirror, he frowned when he noticed the black truck with tinted windows was still two cars behind him. The dark windows had caught his attention, and he made a quick right-hand turn at the next intersection without using his turn signal.

Then he sped up a bit and jockeyed over to the left lane to turn again. The light turned yellow, forcing him to stop and wait.

The black truck with its tinted windows had followed him around the corner and was now only one car back.

Alarm skittered down the back of his neck. He wanted to run the light, but there was too much traffic. The moment he had a green arrow, he made the turn, then executed another left turn at the next street, cutting off a vehicle coming toward him. The driver had to hit the brakes and honked loudly in protest.

"What's happening?" Joy grabbed onto the door handle. "Is someone following us?"

He couldn't lie to her. "Yes, a black truck with tinted windows. Don't worry, I'm going to lose him."

She nodded as he continued making abrupt turns that should have gotten him a reckless-driving ticket. He ended up heading in the opposite direction from where the FBI offices were located, but it couldn't be helped.

Five minutes later, he changed course so that he was back on track. There was no sign now of the black truck with tinted windows.

For now.

But the truck's appearance at all nagged at him. There was no sign of a black truck with tinted windows at the family restaurant or at the American Lodge motel.

So how had he been tagged?

He'd used his phone at the motel and outside the restaurant. If he'd been tracked by using the phone at his motel, shouldn't they have been waiting for them at the restaurant?

It didn't make sense. Unless he was overreacting again and the black truck hadn't belonged to the shooter at all. Maybe the driver of the black truck had mistaken Tarin for someone else.

"Is he gone?"

"Yes. Sorry, I didn't mean to scare you."

"I've told you before, I feel safe with you, Tarin." The way she emphasized the last two words gave him a clue what she was worried about.

"I'm not leaving you at the FBI building. You're stuck with me until we get this guy behind bars."

"What about your job? I know you said you were taking a few days, but this may drag on for a lot longer."

He didn't bother to tell her that his boss had only given him three days off. If this situation with the shooter took longer to be resolved, he'd have some explaining to do.

"The city needs a good detective like you, Tarin," she said softly. "Please don't risk your career for me."

"Hey, I'm going to crack this case with Brady's and Doug's help, and the upper brass will be thrilled to have another case closed," he said lightly. Then he turned serious. "Joy, please believe God has a plan for us. We're going to get through this."

"Okay, you're right. I guess it's hard for me to truly believe that these things happen for a reason."

"They do." He reached over to take her hand again, giving her fingers a gentle squeeze. "Have faith, Joy."

"I have faith in you, Tarin. And in God." She smiled. "Let's do this."

"We will." He no sooner turned right at the next intersection when he noticed the black truck with tinted windows behind him again.

What in the world was going on?

Fearing his phone was somehow hacked, Tarin considered tossing it out. But instead, he called Brady. "I picked up a tail." He kept his voice calm with an effort.

"Where are you?" Brady asked.

"I'm still ten minutes away, but I'm not sure we'll make it." He kept his attention focused on the road. "Don't mention this call to anyone."

"You think there's a leak within the FBI?" Brady sounded incredulous.

Tarin didn't know what to think. He wasn't close enough to the FBI building to head there, so he decided to go toward his precinct instead. He took an abrupt turn through a corner gas station and onto another street.

The black truck did the same thing.

Not good.

"Tarin, what's going on?" Joy sounded scared. Unfortunately, he didn't have time to reassure her.

"Brady, I don't know what's happening, but this guy is definitely following us." He made another abrupt turn. "I'm heading to the precinct."

"I'll meet you there," Brady offered.

"Thanks. Just you, though. Not Bridges, understand?"

"I think you're off base, but I'll come alone," Brady reassured him. "Just make sure you make it in one piece."

"That's the plan." He didn't dare glance at Joy who'd sucked in a harsh breath at his brother's words. He disconnected from the call. If his phone was being tracked, maybe it would help him to show up at the precinct.

Another glance at the rearview mirror proved the truck was still back there. He'd need to resort to drastic measures to shake it.

Thankfully, he and Joy were buckled in. He hit the gas, surging through a red light, then took another left-hand turn with a flashing yellow light, narrowly missing the rear end of a delivery van. Honking horns reverberated around them, but he ignored the annoyed drivers, desperate to put more distance between them and the black truck.

Joy softly murmured the Lord's Prayer, and he found himself repeating the words in the back of his mind as he continued driving like a maniac through the city.

He'd been doing well until he came across a train. A really long train.

Slowing to a stop, he slammed his hand on the steering wheel. He couldn't just sit there, they needed to move. He quickly yanked the gear shift into reverse and shot backward, then turned around and headed back the way they'd come.

When he saw the black truck up ahead coming toward him, he made a quick right turn and punched the gas. He shot down the street, taking every zigzag turn he could manage without hitting a parked or moving car.

After another ten minutes, he was certain he'd shaken

the tail. And as if God was watching over them, a local precinct came into view.

He didn't hesitate to pull into the parking lot. He glanced at Joy. "Are you okay?"

"I—yes." Her voice was barely a whisper.

"Come on. We'll get inside and call my brother." He quickly ushered her out of the truck and covered her back as they headed into the police station.

Inside the lobby, he called Brady. "I need you to meet me at the Timberland Falls police station."

"Why are you there?"

"The black truck with tinted windows found me again." For all Tarin knew, the truck was driving by the police station right now. "Come pick us up, okay?"

"On it," Brady said.

Tarin slid his phone into his pocket. Joy slipped her arm around his waist as if needing support. He hugged her, but his mind was whirling with unanswered questions.

How had the black truck found them? His phone? But that meant someone knew he was involved in the case.

He and Brady had spoken to DEA Agent Doug Bridges, so that was where his first thought went. But then he realized he'd also spoken to his partner, Dave, and his partner had asked about the file yesterday too.

Both were men he should have been able to trust. But right now? He didn't trust anyone but his family.

CHAPTER TEN

Joy didn't think her heart rate would ever return to normal. She'd held on to the door handle so tightly her fingers cramped. Tarin had driven like they'd been racing in the Grand Prix, nearly slamming into other vehicles or being struck by someone else along the way.

"Can I help you?" An officer sitting behind a glass window eyed them warily.

Tarin stepped forward, holding up his badge. "Detective Tarin Finnegan from the MPD Seventh Precinct. Sorry to drop in, but we were followed by a black truck with tinted windows. Ms. Joy Munson here has been a victim of several shooting incidents."

"Shooting incidents?" The officer's eyebrows rose. "Here? I'll have one of our detectives come talk to you."

"Not here," Tarin quickly corrected. "No need to bother a detective. I just needed a safe place to stay. My brother Brady Finnegan is an FBI agent. He'll be here to pick us up."

"I'll still have a detective come talk to you." The officer

picked up the phone, spoke into it, then replaced the receiver. "Detective Kirkus will be right out."

Tarin groaned but nodded. She glanced at him. "Is that a problem?"

"Not exactly, but I don't want to be stuck here explaining everything to him. I don't need more people involved in this. The minute Brady shows up, we're out of here."

She understood his concern about not wanting to be held up here indefinitely.

Detective Kirkus was a woman who looked to be in her forties. "Would you like to come back to my desk so we can talk privately?"

"I'm armed," Tarin said bluntly. "It's better to stay here. I don't think there's anything you'll be able to do, I didn't get the license plate number of the black truck. I was too busy driving like a maniac to lose him."

Detective Kirkus frowned. "And you're sure he was following you?"

"Yes. I lost him several times, but then he'd show up again. Almost as if he knew where I'd be." Tarin's scowl deepened. "I'm sorry, but I can't really go into any more detail. All I'm asking for is some professional courtesy. We'd like to stay here until my brother arrives. I promise we'll be out of your hair soon."

"If there's some guy stalking people in the area, it's important for us to find him." Detective Kirkus did not look happy. "I'd really like a full statement from you."

"Detective, the problem is that I'm in grave danger," Joy said, deflecting the detective's attention from Tarin. "Right now, we're looking for safety. We have the FBI involved. I wish I could give you more information on the black truck, too, but everything happened so fast."

"I can tell you that it looked like a Ford F-150," Tarin said. "If you want to put a BOLO out for it, that works. But I doubt the driver is hanging around now that we're here in the police station with you."

Detective Kirkus stared at Tarin for a long moment. "Okay, fine. You can wait here for your ride. But I would ask for some professional courtesy in return. If you think there's a threat to our community, I need you to tell me."

"I promise I will do that. I honestly don't believe the threat is aimed at anyone except me and Ms. Munson." Tarin shrugged. "The sooner we're out of here, the safer everyone else in the area will be."

The female detective nodded curtly and turned away. Joy let out a soundless sigh of relief that Detective Kirkus hadn't pushed the issue. Although she didn't fully understand why Tarin was worried about explaining the extent of the danger dogging their footsteps.

In her mind, the more people who knew, the better to keep them protected. That way, if something bad did happen, there would be no confusing her death with a freak accident.

The door to the precinct opened. Tarin spun to face the door, his hand resting on his gun. A small elderly woman nearly fell backward in surprise at seeing him there.

"Sorry, ma'am." Tarin smiled reassuringly. "You startled me."

"You startled me," the feisty woman shot back.

"Yes, ma'am. Please accept my apology."

"Hrmph." The woman continued up to the desk. "I'd like to report a robbery. Someone stole my packages off my porch this morning."

Joy couldn't help but admire the woman, but Tarin's

attention was focused outside. "Come on, Brady," he murmured.

"He'll be here soon." She sensed the tension radiating from him.

He smiled at her, then put his arm around her. "You've been amazing through all of this."

He was the one who was amazing, but she managed to hold her tongue. There was no point in letting him know how much she cared about him. Especially since she knew he took his role of protecting her seriously.

It was his job after all.

After another five minutes passed, Tarin's phone rang. He pushed the talk button. "Brady? Great, we'll be right out." He lowered his phone and urged her to the door. "Brady has a black SUV, much like Rhy's."

She nodded, seeing the vehicle parked directly in front of the police station. She and Tarin hurried out. She scooted into the back seat while Tarin jumped into the passenger side.

"What happened?" Brady demanded.

"I'll fill you in, but we need to make sure someone picks up Aiden's truck. Not Elly or Alanna, though, it's too dangerous."

"Rhy and Quinn can do it," Brady said. "Quinn is back from his training stint with the Coast Guard."

"Good. I was hoping we could swap vehicles, but for now, we need to stick together." Tarin opened the passenger-side window and tossed his phone out. Joy gasped as it shattered on the ground, splitting into dozens of pieces. "First thing on the agenda is to pick up disposable phones for me and Joy."

"Okay, what is this about?" Brady demanded. "You really believe someone is tracking your phone?"

"Are you going to tell me that's not possible?" Tarin asked. "Because I find it strange that after I make a few calls, one to my partner and to you where we had a three-way conversation with Agent Doug Bridges that a black truck with tinted windows shows up on my tail."

Brady let out a low whistle. "That does seem suspicious."

"The worst part is I lost the tail several times, only to have the truck reappear out of nowhere. As if the driver knew where to find me." Tarin raked his hand through his hair. "I'm telling you, there's more to this case than we know."

"Okay, I believe you." Brady checked his rearview mirror, giving her a reassuring smile. "We'll stop and pick up a set of disposable phones, but if you think Bridges is involved, we need to get a new vehicle, one without ties to either of us."

"You're right, we do." Tarin sighed. "Maybe we can meet up with Quinn."

"I was thinking more along the lines of borrowing a vehicle that isn't registered to a Finnegan," Brady said. "Kyleigh mentioned a vehicle the sheriff's department recently acquired, an unmarked Jeep. Let's see if we can borrow it for a while."

"That would be good," Tarin agreed. "Although I'd hate for Kyleigh to get in trouble over this."

"She can handle it," Brady said. "Remember how she helped us support Rhy last month? We tend to see her as our sister without giving her credit for being a very capable and skilled sheriff's deputy."

"You're right. She would want to be involved." Tarin turned to look at her. "I'm sorry, Joy, but I only trust my family."

"I understand." Now it all made sense. Tarin was concerned that either the DEA or his partner was someone involved in the drug scheme. It seemed incredible, why would anyone within law enforcement do such a thing? It would sound over-the-top paranoid if not for what she and Tarin had just experienced.

The black truck with tinted windows had found them several times. Either by tracking Tarin's phone or because he knew where they were going.

She shivered and tried to fight a wave of overwhelming despair. Without help from either the FBI or the DEA, how would they figure out who's behind these attacks?

Obviously, she trusted his family. But could they do this alone? She was very much afraid that without access to law enforcement resources, they'd never get to the bottom of this mess.

And as much as she cared about Tarin, she desperately wanted her boring and mundane life back.

One thing she'd learned through all of this. Living on the edge was not for her.

TARIN DIDN'T FEEL safe until they'd stopped by the sheriff's department to pick up the Jeep arranged for them by Kyleigh. She was working downtown at the courthouse but had helped with the swap.

"Next stop, a big box store for phones," Tarin said.

"On it," Brady agreed. "Then where?"

Tarin hesitated. It was a good question. They still had a room at the American Lodge. Thinking back to the sequence of events, he didn't believe their position had been compromised until he'd made those calls at breakfast.

It wasn't likely the shooter knew about the American Lodge.

Yet going back to the same place was a risk.

"We need a new location," he finally said. "Someplace no one would think to search for us. So that means nothing in Brookland or in Oakdale."

"Okay, there's a place called Windmill Inn," Brady suggested. "I think it's far enough off the beaten track to work for you and Joy."

Tarin had never heard of it. "Okay, but I hope they take cash. It's one of the reasons we tend to use Gary Campbell's place."

"I'll make that happen," Brady assured him. "But we need to talk this through. I highly doubt Doug is dirty, and we really could use support from the DEA on this."

"Nope, not going to trust him." Tarin was not going to budge on this point. "However, I will need you to access the FBI database to see what if anything you can find on Dr. Eli Lewis, pharmacist Craig Washington, and any other known associates."

"Okay, but know that I don't have the creds to access the DEA information." Brady pulled into the parking lot of a store. "Looks like they're just opening now. Why don't you and Joy wait here while I get the phones?"

"Grab a computer too," Tarin said. "Thanks."

"You got it." Brady slid from the Jeep and disappeared inside the store.

"Tarin, how are we going to do this?" Joy's voice cracked a bit. "I'm very afraid we'll never get to the bottom of these attacks without help from law enforcement. Especially the DEA."

Tarin shifted in his seat to face her. "I know it's scary, and I wish there was another option. I know my partner,

Dave, is aware of my intent to reopen your brother's case, and I shared similar concerns with Agent Bridges. One of them is likely involved. And for now, they're both off-limits until I can figure out which one is dirty."

She swallowed hard and looked away. "I'm trying to be strong, but it feels like I'll never be safe."

"You're safe with me and Brady." He hated seeing her so upset. "Don't underestimate the Finnegans. We know how to uncover the truth."

Swiping at her eyes, she nodded. He ached to pull her into his arms, but being in the Jeep made that impossible. Which was for the best, anyway, as he needed to keep his head screwed on straight.

Tarin leaned toward Doug Bridges being the bad apple, mostly because he wanted to believe his partner was clean. He'd worked with Dave for five years. He'd know if the guy was dirty.

Then again, Dave was somewhat reserved, never getting too close. After the way he'd lost Caroline, that distance had been fine with him.

But now it made him wonder. Dave had been with him at the scene of Ken's death, instantly taking the stance that it was a suicide. Considering the note, the empty pill bottle, and the ME's report, it wasn't a stretch.

But now that quick conclusion made him wonder.

Brady returned with the electronics. "We're set. Oh, and Quinn called when I was in the store. He and a buddy are heading out to get Aiden's truck."

"Good, but what about your SUV?"

Brady shrugged. "I can always take a rideshare back to the sheriff's department to pick up my car. If Bridges is involved, it will look suspicious if I'm not driving my usual vehicle."

The whole mess was giving him a headache. "Smart, I don't want to raise concerns with Doug Bridges. And what about Marc Callahan? Are you sure you can trust him?"

"Yes, Marc is a good guy," Brady said. "He gave me Bridges's contact information based on a case from two years ago. Marc was only peripherally involved. You know what Elly said, the entire Callahan family is similar to ours in that they're all dedicated to community service, mostly law enforcement as well as Maddy Sinclair being an assistant district attorney."

"Yeah, I remember." Tarin did his best to rein in his overactive imagination. He needed to stay focused rather than seeing boogeymen around every corner. "It helps to know Callahan isn't close friends with Doug Bridges."

"I can see if there's another DEA agent we can work with," Brady suggested.

"Let's hold off for now. Where is this Windmill Inn anyway?"

"A little farther west, but only ten minutes via the interstate." Brady hit the gas as they reached the freeway on-ramp.

"Keep an eye out for the black Ford F-150 with tinted windows," Tarin said wearily. "If Bridges is the leak, he may have tapped into your phone."

"I will," Brady said grimly.

Thankfully, there was no sign of the black truck. The Windmill Inn was smaller than the American Lodge, but Tarin didn't care as long as it was clean and they accepted cash.

Brady secured the connecting rooms. They weren't bad, so Tarin quickly went to work activating the new phones while Brady set up the new computer. The motel provided free Wi-Fi, which also helped.

"What can I do to help?" Joy asked.

"All you need to do is rest and relax," Tarin told her. "We're safe here."

"We were supposed to be safe at the FBI offices by now too," she pointed out dryly.

"True." Tarin felt as if he'd let her down. "That should have been the safest place of all. I'm sorry it didn't work out that way."

"It's not your fault." She blew out a breath. "Sorry, I don't mean to be cranky."

"You're not," Tarin assured her.

"I'm in," Brady said. "I added the extra security software so I can access the FBI database remotely."

Tarin was still working on the phones. "See if there's anything on Craig Washington, he's a pharmacist."

"Technically, he's a PharmD," Joy said. When Brady lifted an eyebrow, she added, "That means he's earned a doctorate degree in pharmacology from University of Wisconsin – Madison."

Tarin finished with the phones, handing one to Joy. "Keep it with you, I've programmed my number in your phone."

"Great, thanks." Joy sighed. "At some point, I'll need to call my boss."

"Not yet," Tarin cautioned.

"Same goes for you, I assume," she said.

He nodded. "You bet. I'm not using this phone to contact anyone at the precinct."

She seemed reassured by the news.

"Let's see what you have, Brady." Tarin gestured for Joy to join them, crowding around his brother so they could see what came up on the screen.

"Okay, I found a report on the arrest of Dr. Eli Lewis."

Brady tapped several keys to bring the document up larger so they could all read it. "You were right, Joy, he's been arrested for writing fraudulent scripts to the tune of ten thousand of them, and those are just the ones they know about."

"If each script is worth twenty dollars, that's two hundred thousand dollars," Tarin said. "But they found millions in his offshore accounts, right?"

"That's correct. But keep in mind, these prescriptions are good for a year," Joy spoke up. "The one found in Ken's bedroom said there were nine refills left."

Tarin nodded slowly. "If the average refill is one per month, that adds lots more zeros onto that equation."

"The pills themselves are dirt cheap," Brady said. "At least, according to Doug Bridges. He also told me that just five Percocet tablets on the street is easily worth twenty bucks. I'm sure the pharmacy was selling a thirty-day supply for more than that. Not to mention, they'd get a cut of the profits too. Maybe not as high as the doc, but enough to make it worth their while."

"So maybe fifty bucks per refill," Tarin said. "That would explain the millions of dollars squirreled away in Lewis's accounts."

"For sure," Brady agreed.

"That helps explain why someone is trying to kill me," Joy whispered.

"Hey, no one will find you here." Tarin draped a casual arm around her shoulders. "And maybe we'll find another thread to tug to unravel this case."

"I just hope that person isn't dead, like Leon." She sighed and leaned against him.

"Leon?" Brady asked.

"Leon Webber, he's a pharmacy tech who used to work

for Craig Washington. He was killed in a car crash a year after Joy's brother Ken died of a staged suicide. Different counties, so the fact that they both worked at the same pharmacy slipped through the cracks."

"Not to mention, the killer made sure Ken's death looked like a suicide. Nothing suspicious about that," Joy added dryly.

"That's too much of a coincidence for me." Brady turned back to the report. "I can pull up Leon Webber's report, see if there's anything that raises a red flag now that we know the truth."

"I don't see anything helpful in this report," Tarin said, scanning the page. "Unless I'm missing something."

"You're not, although the DEA agent listed here is James Turban." Brady's expression was thoughtful. "I wonder if we should call him?"

"Not yet." Tarin knew he sounded like a broken record, repeating his same concerns over and over. "Let's see what you can find on Craig Washington."

"Okay." Brady minimized the report and put Washington's name in the database. After a moment, he said, "Looks like his name came up in the Lewis investigation, but there's no indication that he was looked at in more depth."

"Why not?" Joy asked. "I'd think Craig would be guilty of not using the pharmacy database that is supposed to flag providers who are overprescribing. According to my brother, Ken, the pharmacist can get in just as much trouble as the provider."

"I'm not sure why they didn't dig into Washington," Brady admitted. "The DEA agent is the same one, James Turban."

If Turban was the agent involved in the scheme, why had the black truck shown up after his conversation with

Bridges? Even he wasn't paranoid enough to believe there was a cadre of dirty DEA agents. Even one dirty cop was unusual. Despite what some TV shows portrayed, 99 percent of all cops were decent, hardworking people who cared about keeping the community safe.

"Hang on, let me try another database." Brady went to work on the keyboard. Tarin appreciated his brother's willingness to share whatever intel the feds had, even though so far they hadn't learned anything new.

Having Joy so close was also proving to be a distraction. If Brady wasn't sitting right there, he might have given in to the temptation to kiss her.

"Okay, here's something." Brady's excited tone pulled him back to the case. "Looks like Craig Washington was reprimanded for filling the prescriptions by Dr. Eli Lewis, Dr. Steve Armond, Dr. Jeffery Quincy, and Dr. Fred Newman, who, as it turned out, were all aliases with different DEA numbers for Eli Lewis. Craig argued that there was no way for him to know the doctors were all the same person, so the state backed off and decided not to take any further action against his license."

"That's why he wasn't arrested," Joy said. "But Tarin and I were at his pharmacy, there's no way he wasn't aware of what was going on."

"I agree with Joy," Tarin said. "And if Agent James Turban had bothered to stake out the pharmacy, he'd know that too."

"It looks like they went down the path of building the case against Lewis, shutting down all the alias DEA numbers he was using." Brady scowled. "How can Craig still be filling prescriptions without Lewis or one of his fake doctor's writing them?"

"Good question. Presumably some other doc stepped into Eli Lewis's place."

Joy asked, "Can the FBI access Craig's Corner Pharmacy records?"

"Not without a warrant." But then Brady brightened. "Maybe we can access them for an ongoing investigation. Since Eli Lewis hasn't accepted a plea deal yet, we may be able to use that to get more information from the pharmacy we know was involved."

Tarin put a hand on his brother's arm. "I would love to see those records but don't do something that will get you into trouble. The DEA has jurisdiction over this case, not regular FBI."

"That's not entirely true." Brady went back to work on the keyboard. "The attempts against Joy have happened in multiple police districts. Under that circumstance, the FBI can assist in coordinating the investigation."

"Sounds like a stretch," Tarin protested.

"I don't want anyone to get in trouble over me," Joy added. "It's bad enough I'm forcing you to spend money on vehicles, motel rooms, food, etc."

"Hey, we live for this stuff," Brady joked. Then his expression turned serious. "Okay, give me a few minutes to pull some information."

Tarin sat back in his chair, hoping and praying Brady's career wouldn't suffer over this. It was one thing for him to risk his rank as a detective, but he would never ask the same from his siblings.

"Hey, I found something," Brady said.

"Already?" Tarin frowned.

"Yeah, a report from Craig's Corner was already in the system. It was pulled two days ago. And it looks like the report was authorized by DEA Agent Doug Bridges."

Tarin stared at the screen, trying to understand what that meant. Was Bridges trying to do the right thing, investigating the pharmacy when James Turban hadn't?

Or was Bridges trying to cover his tracks because he's involved in this mess?

CHAPTER ELEVEN

"I find it hard to believe Agent Bridges is involved in this." Joy wished she could stay close to Tarin forever, but of course, that wasn't an option. She moved away enough to meet his gaze. "Why would he do that when his job is to eliminate illegal drugs?"

"Why does any cop go bad?" Tarin shrugged. "Money. I hate to say it, but greed has no bounds."

Working as an internal auditor, she'd stumbled across more than one instance of someone misappropriating funds. But moving money from one account to another seemed different from supporting illegal prescriptions, knowing you were contributing to those who were addicted to pain meds. Maybe fighting the war against drugs got old, and the DEA agent had decided it was easier and more lucrative to play along.

"I'm not sure Bridges is a bad guy," Brady countered. He was scrolling through the report on the computer. "This report shows very clearly the high amounts of narcotics going through Craig's Corner Pharmacy. There are several different doctors' names listed too. That's the same thing that happened with Eli Lewis."

Joy frowned. "But if Bridges isn't a bad agent, how were we found so quickly by the black truck with tinted windows?"

"I'm not ready to trust Bridges yet," Tarin said grimly. "Although we need to consider my partner, Dave, may be involved. I hate thinking the worst about him, but I did call Dave from the restaurant."

Joy remembered Dave from when he and Tarin had investigated Ken's death. Back then, she'd thought him a good cop. Tarin had taken the lead role, though, and it was clear to her that Tarin was the one with more experience. "How long was Dave a detective before he became your partner?"

"Not long, he was new and was assigned to me after I lost Caroline." Tarin shrugged. "I have to be honest, I never had the slightest inkling that he might be dirty. Maybe a bit too laid-back and not as motivated to work extra, but not on the take."

"Maybe we're missing some other connection," Brady said thoughtfully. "You had your phone, so maybe someone with excellent tech skills was able to hack into it to learn your location. It wouldn't be a stretch for that person to see where your vehicle was going and follow."

"I assumed that was someone with cop resources," Tarin admitted. "But you are right that it could be anyone."

Joy had a crazy thought. "Kevin used to work for the IT department at Trinity Medical Center. We could call him to get more information on how difficult it might be to hack into phones."

Tarin turned to look at her. "I'd forgotten he worked in

IT at the hospital. But I'm not sure I want to call him either. The less people involved at this point, the better."

"Okay, but what are we going to do?" She couldn't hide her frustration. "We can't just hang out in a motel room indefinitely."

"No, we can't." Tarin gestured to the computer screen. "Maybe we can find something to go on in the report."

"I'd like to take a look at it." Joy lifted a hand as the two Finnegans looked as if they wanted to argue. "I'm accustomed to looking at data and picking out patterns. It's probably the only skill I can bring to this investigation."

Brady and Tarin exchanged a glance. She could tell Brady was leaving the decision to Tarin.

"That's fine with me," Tarin agreed.

"Great." She reached out to turn the laptop toward her. "It would help if you guys would back off, I'm not used to working with someone peering over my shoulder."

Tarin and Brady both stood and left her alone. The two men went over to the connecting room, she could hear their muted voices in the background. But that was fine, she easily tuned out the sound and focused on the report from Craig's Corner Pharmacy.

The columns of data were overwhelming at first, but as she began sorting the spreadsheet by different categories, the patterns she'd anticipated began to emerge. Elbow deep in spreadsheets was her comfort zone, and she had no idea how long she'd been working when Tarin set a cup of coffee at her elbow.

"Oh, thanks." Distracted, she glanced up at him, then reached for the coffee. She was touched that he'd doctored it the way she liked. "I've narrowed the list to the prescriptions I believe are fraudulent."

"You have?" Tarin dropped beside her. His musky scent

made her want to smile for no reason other than he was there.

"Ah, yes." *Focus*, she told herself firmly. "They're using the same scheme Eli Lewis used. In this spreadsheet, I sorted by patient name. You can easily see those getting prescriptions are from one of five doctors' names. I'm not sure how the narcotic database works, but I'm assuming Craig knows how to avoid being flagged by the system."

"That's amazing." Tarin's praise for her work warmed her heart. "And you did that so quickly."

"I did?" She glanced at the clock. Only a half hour had passed. "Here's the thing that's bothering me, though. I feel like one pharmacy isn't enough."

Tarin cocked his head. "What do you mean?"

"We can do the running total here on how much money is moving through Craig's Corner, and while it's significant, the profits are split between the doc and the pharmacist, right?"

"Right."

"If there was more than one pharmacy, owned by Craig Washington under his name or a fake name, the profits would double." She spread her hands. "Maybe it's me, but while the money is impressive, I find it hard to believe it's enough to risk killing people over. Crossing the line to murder raises the stakes of getting caught."

"It does, but so far they've made the deaths look like an accident and/or suicide." Tarin rubbed his chin. "But you do have a point. Brady?" He called to his brother, who joined them from the connecting room. "Can we use the federal database to see if Craig Washington has any other pharmacies under his name or a corporate name?"

"Sure." Brady looked intrigued by the idea. "If you're finished with the computer, I'll see what I can find."

"Let me save these files." She hit a few keystrokes to preserve her work before standing and moving away to hand the computer over to Brady.

"Did you and your brother come up with anything?" She eyed him curiously. "I heard you talking in the other room."

"We tossed around a couple of ideas," Tarin admitted. "The biggest problem is that we need to bring someone in from the DEA that we can trust."

"Brady can't be the point person? I know he's not DEA, but he's still an FBI agent."

"That's one possibility. He's waiting for a call back from Marc Callahan. We believe we can trust him, and he may have an idea of how we can go up the chain of command to reach someone to talk to."

"I keep thinking about Sue, the pharmacy tech working for Craig. She must be getting something out of this too. Adding people to an illegal scheme means splitting the profits if the goal is to convince them to play along."

"True." Tarin blew out a breath. "Maybe it's time for me to have a chat with her. See if I can't make her understand the error of her ways."

Her stomach clenched, an irrational wave of fear hitting hard. A conversation shouldn't be a precursor to danger, but she didn't like it. "It might be better if I talk to her. Maybe she doesn't realize that Leon and Ken were both murdered to cover up the illegal drugs going through the pharmacy."

"No way." Tarin's expression turned stubborn. "I'm not putting you in harm's way."

"You'll keep me safe, besides, I don't think she'll talk to you, Tarin. No offense, but everything about you screams cop."

The corner of his mouth kicked up in a smile. "None

taken." His smile slowly faded. "But I'm not sure I want you to leave this room."

Joy wished she could use the computer again. "If I remember correctly, each of the techs had to alternate working Saturdays, which meant they had a day off during the week. We know Sue was there yesterday. We should swing by and see if she's there today or if she's off. If she's there, we might be able to catch her during a lunch break."

"You can stay here while I check it out," Tarin said.

"Please, Tarin. I was able to get some information out of her yesterday. Give me another chance."

It was obvious he didn't like it, but Brady piped up. "I think you should go together, Tarin. Marc Callahan is picking me up here in about fifteen minutes. We'll talk through the case with him, then you and Joy can head out to speak with Sue. We'll follow, setting up someplace close by to make sure things don't go south."

That information was enough to sway Tarin. "Okay."

Brady continued working on the computer, leaving her at loose ends. She was glad she'd been able to participate in a very small way, but they were no closer to finding proof about who had killed her brother and Leon Webber.

And there were the series of attacks against her too. Craig was busy working in his own pharmacy, filling fraudulent scripts, so it was highly unlikely he personally had pulled the trigger.

The gunman was probably a stranger, which would make it that much more difficult to find him.

After freshening up in the bathroom, she returned to find Brady was still at the computer. Tarin had dropped down beside him. Brady was blond, like Rhy, but she'd noticed Tarin's red hair was shared by his sister Elly.

She thought about the Finnegan sisters and how they

must be wondering where Tarin was. She knew Tarin would have connected with Rhy at some point, but still, she felt guilty for keeping him away from the rest of his family.

Tarin was going to great lengths to keep her safe. Watching him in action made her realize he put his life on the line for others every single day.

And that was something that would not be easy to live with on a long-term basis. All the more reason to keep her relationship with Tarin on a friendship level.

She couldn't afford the stress of falling in love with him.

A KNOCK at the door startled Tarin. He jumped up from his seat, his hand going for his weapon, until he realized Brady was looking at him oddly.

"That's probably Callahan. I told you he was coming," Brady said. He crossed over to look through the peephole, then opened the door. "Hey, Marc, thanks for coming."

"Of course." A tall dark-haired man with keen green eyes stepped into the room. The Callahans were as dark as the Finnegans were light. No sign of a family resemblance from the outside. "Obviously, it's not good to hear you believe there's a link within the agency, Brady."

"The DEA," Tarin corrected. He held out his hand. "I'm Detective Tarin Finnegan, Brady's older brother."

"Marc Callahan, nice to meet you. I heard about you from my brother Miles." A smile creased Marc's face. "And, of course, our sister Maddy is all in on the DNA connection between our families."

"Yeah, Elly, our youngest sister, is pretty excited about that too," Tarin admitted. "It's as if having nine siblings wasn't enough for her, she had to go looking for more family."

Marc chuckled. "At least your parents didn't burden you each with names that start with the same letter. I can't tell you how often our parents got our names wrong because they named us Marc, Miles, Mitch, Mike, Matthew, and Maddy."

"That does sound confusing," Brady agreed. "Although our parents goofed up our names plenty before they died."

"Yeah, I heard about how you lost them ten years ago. Please accept my condolences," Marc said.

"Thanks," Brady said with a nod. "Tarin here and our oldest brother, Rhy, kept the family together. They deserve the credit."

Tarin waved that away. He didn't want accolades for doing what was necessary. "We didn't mind, and Rhy did most of the work." He grimaced, then added, "As much as I like hearing about the Callahan family being related to the Finnegans, we need to stay focused on the problem." Tarin reached for her Joy's arm, drawing her into the conversation. "This is Joy Munson, she's been the victim of multiple attacks, and we have a good reason to believe they're all related to the illegal drug scheme being performed out of Craig's Corner Pharmacy."

Marc nodded, his expression turning serious. "I heard, and apparently as soon as you spoke to Doug Bridges of the DEA, you caught a tail."

"We did, and it was hairy there for a moment." *For many long moments*, he silently added, thinking about the terrifying race through the city. "Thankfully, we're safe now, but there isn't time to waste. We need information, proof of some kind that can bring down this illegal drug operation as soon as possible."

"What can I do to help?" Marc asked.

Tarin was touched that the FBI agent agreed to help so quickly. It was a sign that the Callahan DNA was very similar to that of the Finnegan family. "We have a plan, and I was hoping you and Brady would back us up."

"I'm in." Marc spoke without hesitation. "And I have electronics in my car if we need to wire you up."

"A wire?" Tarin was intrigued. He glanced at Joy. "What do you think?"

"I'm game if you think it will help." A brief flash of apprehension darkened her eyes, but then it was gone. "I only hope I can convince Sue to talk."

"What's the plan?" Marc asked.

Tarin quickly filled him in. Marc and Brady both agreed to stake out the pharmacy if Sue was in fact working there. And they'd do the same at her house if she had the day off.

He felt good about taking some action, hopefully convincing Sue to turn on her boss. Something had to break in this case and soon.

"Maybe we should call Craig's Corner, see who answers the phone," Joy suggested. "That's usually the tech's job."

"Good idea, I'll make the call," Brady offered. He stepped into the next room to do so.

"What do you think about going up the ladder at the DEA?" Tarin asked Marc. "Technically, we're stomping all over DEA jurisdiction here."

"I've been thinking about that," Marc admitted. "There is a DEA liaison within the Milwaukee County Sheriff's Office. My brother Mike is a deputy, I'm sure he can link us up with him."

"Our sister Kyleigh is a deputy too, but she's currently stationed down at the courthouse." Tarin nodded slowly. "I like the idea of using the MCSO liaison. But let's see what we can get from the pharmacy tech first."

"I'll text Mike in the meantime, just to let him know we may need his help with the liaison." Marc flashed a smile. "I wonder if he knows your sister."

"I'm sure he does." Tarin couldn't help but grin. "Kinda crazy to realize we've been working alongside our cousins all along."

"Right?" Marc shook his head. "I'm still trying to figure out why we didn't know about the family connection earlier. My mom claims she didn't know about your mother, Colleen, which would have been her cousin. Although I'm not sure why as they shared the same set of grandparents."

Tarin frowned. Trying to follow the tangled branches of the family tree wasn't easy. "Maybe something happened that split the family apart?"

"If so, my mother didn't seem to be aware of it. Although the discord was likely from the previous generation. Who knows?" Marc worked the phone, sending his text. "I'm sure our sisters will get to the bottom of it."

Knowing how stubborn Elly could be when setting her mind to something, Tarin couldn't argue. "They will."

After a moment, Brady returned. "Okay, Sue answered the phone, so she is working today. I asked about a prescription, but she couldn't find it in the database." He shrugged. "Hopefully, that didn't raise her suspicions."

"It might after we confront her, but that's okay," Joy said. "I happen to know the staff at the pharmacy like to take their lunch breaks at the café across the street. At least, they did when Ken worked there."

"That's great information." Tarin went back over to the computer screen and brought up a map of the area. "Which one?"

Joy quickly pinpointed the location. "Here, it's called Baker's Best Café. I guess they specialize in homemade bread and sandwiches." A hint of sadness crossed her features. "Ken raved about them."

He couldn't help putting his arm around her shoulders, giving her a reassuring hug. Of course, Brady noticed, as did Marc, but while their facial expressions spoke volumes, they thankfully kept their mouths shut.

Tarin knew he needed to stop crossing the line with Joy. When he was focused on the case, it was easy to keep their relationship professional.

It was only when she displayed emotions, especially of fear or sorrow, that he couldn't seem to hold back from offering comfort. He just couldn't seem to ignore the impulse to ease her pain.

"Okay, Mike gave me the name of Deputy Grady Norquist." Marc held up his phone. "He's the DEA liaison within the sheriff's department. If Tarin and Joy can convince Sue the pharmacy tech to work with us against Craig, we'll get Norquist involved."

"Good." Tarin liked how the plan was coming together. "We still have a solid sixty minutes until lunchtime, but I think we should get set up at the café. If the food is that good, it will be packed over the noon hour."

"Okay, Marc and I will head in first, we'll grab a table." Brady waved a hand. "I think you and Joy should be at another table, where Joy can watch the doorway for Sue to arrive."

This was the only part of the plan that concerned him. He couldn't argue that Joy was more likely to get Sue to talk, but he didn't like having her out in the open at all. "Okay, but make sure we get a table that's not right next to any windows."

"Yeah, roger that," Brady agreed solemnly. "One attempt at shooting through a café window is more than enough."

As he still had his arm around Joy's shoulders, he felt her shiver. "You don't have to do this," he said quietly. "You can stay here. I can ask one of my brothers to come stay with you."

"No, I think I'll be able to convince Sue to cooperate," Joy said firmly. "I believe she'll listen to me about how Ken's and Leon's deaths were no accident. And how there have been five attempts to kill me too." She lifted her chin, and he was impressed with her courage despite her fear.

"You're a brave woman, Joy," he said. "And know that all three of us will do everything possible to protect you."

"Absolutely," Marc agreed.

"Ditto," Brady added, striving for a light tone. "Let's get you wired for sound, shall we?"

Five minutes later, Joy had the wire taped to her blouse beneath her sweater. After testing the equipment worked, Brady nodded. "Okay, you're ready to rumble. We'll head out first using Marc's vehicle. Take the Jeep keys, Tarin." Brady tossed them into the air so he could grab them. "Give us about ten minutes to get situated before you and Joy show up."

"That's fine. We're going to take a convoluted route anyway," Tarin agreed. He packed up the computer and handed it to Brady. "You may want to do more digging while you guys are waiting for the main event."

"Nah, we're going to eat," Marc joked. "I'm hungry."

"It's not as if we haven't worked while eating before," Brady said dryly, throwing the computer bag over his shoulder. "I'll let you buy me lunch."

"Me? I thought you'd spring for the meal," Marc complained.

"I suppose I should since you're helping us out." Brady sighed. "Okay, this one is on me. But next time, you're up."

"Challenge accepted," Marc said with a grin.

Tarin waited for the two FBI agents to leave, thinking it was a little scary how Marc Callahan felt like one of the family. Granted, he was a second cousin, but even without that DNA discovery, the guy fit right in.

As no doubt the rest of the Callahans would too. Maybe having additional family members wouldn't be such a bad thing. At times like this, every helping hand was an added advantage.

Tarin gave the feds a solid five minutes before heading out to Brady's SUV. Joy's expression was a bit apprehensive, but she smiled as she buckled her seat belt, making sure not to dislodge the wire.

"You family is great, Tarin. And I like Marc Callahan too."

"I can't argue," Tarin said lightly. "I trust them to cover our backs." He backed out of the motel parking lot, then headed east. The pharmacy was only about fifteen minutes away, so there was plenty of time to make sure he didn't have a tail before reaching the café.

Thankfully, there was no sign of the black truck with tinted windows or any other vehicle tailing them that he could see. Still, he backtracked twice, going north several miles before turned back to head in the proper direction.

Joy was quiet on the drive, as if marshaling her thoughts. He didn't want to pressure her too much, but this was probably their one and only chance to convince Sue to give up her boss.

Twenty-five minutes later, he found a place to park a

block from the café. Tarin didn't see anything concerning, but even walking one block was enough to put his nerves on edge. "Remember, we act like we don't know Marc and Brady."

"I know." Joy reached for his hand. "Thanks for your support, Tarin."

"Anytime." He opened the door for her, noticing that Marc and Brady were sitting at a table near the front window. When he noticed an empty table in the corner, far away from the windows, he realized they'd purposefully left that one for him and Joy.

"I'll order us some food, what would you like?"

"Turkey sandwich on whole grain bread."

He stood in line to get their meals, then carried the wrapped sandwiches and two bottles of water to the table. The time was quarter to twelve, so he didn't immediately unwrap his sandwich. "Let's wait to see if Sue arrives."

"Okay." Joy took a sip of her water, her eyes glued to the door.

The minutes ticked by slowly. He didn't like sitting without a direct line of sight to the door, but it was better for Joy to see Sue first. Besides, his brother and Marc could see the doorway too.

"She's coming," Joy said breathlessly. She took another swig of her water and stood. "I'm going to see if I can get her to come over to our table."

Tarin knew Marc and Brady could hear Joy's comments, so they'd be ready if the initial meeting didn't go as planned. Joy took a deep breath and made her way through the crowded café toward the door.

To her credit, she didn't so much as glance at Brady or Marc. Her eyes were focused on Sue opening the door and stepping inside. Tarin could hear the conversation too.

"Joy, what are you doing here?" Sue frowned deeply and moved to brush past her

"Ken's death and Leon's were not accidents. And someone is trying to kill me," Joy said quickly. "Please, I need you to talk to me and Tarin. Five minutes, Sue. This is serious."

Sue stood indecisively for a long moment. Before she could say a word, the glass of the door shattered as a bullet plowed through, striking Sue in the center of her back. She fell forward, nearly hitting Joy before landing hard on the floor. A pool of blood formed beneath her.

"Down, everyone down!" Brady shouted, lunging toward Joy, protecting her with his body. Tarin ran forward to join them, his mind whirling.

Their key witness had just been shot!

CHAPTER TWELVE

Joy would never forget the look on Sue's face when the bullet had struck her from behind. The utter shock, disbelief, and maybe a flash of resignation as she fell forward, hitting the floor.

There was so much blood. Too much to give her hope that Sue would survive.

Brady covered her with his body, the way Tarin would have, as the café patrons ducked beneath their tables. Shouts and screams reverberated through the restaurant.

"Are you hurt?" Tarin asked as he crouched beside her. Marc joined them until there was a ring of men surrounding her.

Protecting her.

"Fine." She wasn't fine, but she wasn't injured either. The blood staining her sweater belonged to Sue.

"She's dead," Marc said grimly from his position beside the fallen pharmacy tech. He called for backup as the scene continued to erupt into chaos.

"Anyone see the shooter?" Tarin asked, glancing around. None of the customers paid him any attention.

"I'm a detective with the MPD!" Tarin shouted again. Now some of the crying and shouting quieted down.

"And I'm FBI Agent Finnegan," Brady added, holding up his badge. "Did anyone see the shooter?"

Now the place fell silent as they all looked at each other, waiting for someone to answer.

No one did.

"I'm going outside," Marc said. "I'm sure the guy is long gone, but I'm going to check anyway."

"Go," Brady said. "But be careful."

Marc nodded, pulled his weapon, and moved toward the door, shards of glass crunching beneath his shoes. Joy stared at the glass fragments spread far and wide, thinking this was the third time she'd been surrounded by broken glass in two days.

As if her entire life was in pieces like those shards of glass. Never to be put back together.

"Do you think he was aiming at me?" The question popped out of her mouth before she could stop it. "Sue may have gotten in his way."

"No, I think the shooter intended to kill Sue before she could talk to us." Tarin's voice was grim. "But the real question is, how did he know we were here? We weren't followed, and we don't have phones that can be easily tracked."

She shook her head, feeling helpless. Sue was lying face down, a pool of blood spreading from beneath her. It was one thing to know she was a target because she'd poked her nose into her brother's death, but the way Sue had been ruthlessly murdered indicated the shooter was getting desperate.

Squads pulled up, lights flashing. Brady stood and headed out to talk with them. Tarin remained crouched in front of her, his body blocking hers from the doorway. It didn't take long for both Marc and Brady to come back inside.

"No sign of the shooter," Marc said, his tone full of disgust. "But I did find another shell casing." He held up an evidence bag.

"That's two now," Tarin said, rising to his feet and drawing her up with him. "There was a shell casing found near the bank café shooting site too. It would be good to know if they match."

"Agreed," Brady said. "We'll check on that ASAP. In the meantime, we need to make sure you and Joy are safe."

"That's impossible," she said wearily. "This proves I won't be safe until this guy is caught."

Brady's smile didn't reach his eyes. "Tarin will keep you safe, Joy. And we're going to find this guy. He's making mistakes that will eventually lead us to him."

She didn't think he'd made many mistakes. Two shell casings wouldn't help. Nothing would help. A wave of despair almost sent her to her knees. She hated the violence that surrounded her, that dogged her every step, without any sign of stopping.

Why, Lord, why?

Her silent cry went unanswered.

"We need to get to Sue's house ASAP," Tarin said. "She may have evidence there that can help us."

"Marc is on it," Brady agreed. "We have her full name, Sue Melius, and her address. As soon as we get you two safely back to the motel, we're heading over. Officers are there now to secure the scene."

The possibility of finding evidence at Sue's home helped calm her frayed nerves. "You think there's something that can pinpoint Craig Washington as being the driving force behind this?"

"It's possible," Brady said with a nod.

"Okay, we'll get out of here as soon as we've given our statements," Tarin agreed. She could tell he was anxious to get moving. "Where's the sergeant in charge?"

"Here," a voice drawled. "I'm Sargent Noah Sinclair." The sergeant nodded at them, his brown gaze softening a bit when he saw the blood on her sweater. "Tarin and Brady, right? I met your brother Rhy about a month ago. Seems danger is following the Finnegan family."

"That's the nature of the job, isn't it?" Brady asked.

"True, but I've been on the other side too. Two years ago, when Maddy was in danger, we had to go on the run to survive."

The name clicked in Joy's mind. Maddy was the Callahan who was working on the DNA connection with Elly. "You're Marc's brother-in-law?"

"Guilty," Noah said with a wry grin. Then his expression turned serious. "Can you tell me what happened?"

She stared at him for a moment, trying to gather her thoughts. "I honestly didn't see much. I was moving forward to speak to Sue, when she abruptly stopped, frowning at me as if she wasn't happy to see me. I told her why I was there, that my brother's death and the other pharmacy tech Leon's car crash were both the result of murder. I stepped to the side, indicating she should come to our table, when the door window shattered, and Sue fell forward, hitting the floor." She glanced down at her blood-stained sweater. "I—that's all I remember. I didn't see anything else."

"I'm sorry you had to witness that," Noah said sympathetically. He turned toward Tarin. "What about you?"

"I was several feet behind Joy, and my attention was

focused on her and Sue." He grimaced. "I should have expected something like this."

"Why do you say that?" Noah asked.

"We've been stymied on this case at every turn. It's almost as if this guy knows what we're planning next. I'm not sure how, but whoever the shooter is, he's good."

"Maybe not that good," Brady said. "After losing track of you and Joy, it's not a stretch for this guy to plan on staking out the pharmacy, hoping you'd show."

"But if that's true, why not take a shot at us?" Tarin asked, frustration lining his voice. "Why kill Sue?"

"Craig may have been inside the pharmacy when you made the call about the prescription." Joy put a hand on Tarin's arm. "If he was suspicious and worried about what Sue might say, he could have called the gunman to take care of her."

"Joy is right, Craig may have realized Sue was the weak link in the scheme." Brady shrugged. "We'll know more when we get to her place."

"Do you need us for anything else, Noah?" Tarin asked. "We need to get Joy somewhere safe."

"I'll work with the officers to interview the rest of the patrons." Noah gestured to them with his hand. "How can I get in touch with you if I have more questions?"

"Go through me," Brady said, handing him his card. "I'll get you connected with Tarin. He and Joy are staying off-grid."

"Okay, that works." Noah pocketed the card. "Thanks."

Joy forced herself to step away from Sue. There was nothing she could do for the woman now.

"Brady, the Jeep is a block away," Tarin said. "I'm not sure if it's within the perimeter established by the officers."

"We'll get you out of here," Brady assured them.

True to his word, Marc and Brady were able to get the SUV out of the parking space, which was inside the police perimeter. Joy nervously glanced around the sea of police officers, wondering if the gunman was really gone or hiding nearby.

Sticking around wouldn't be smart, but if he had police connections, either through the DEA or the Milwaukee Police Department, she felt certain he'd try to blend in.

"I hope he's not watching us," she murmured in a low voice to Tarin. "Especially if he's a cop."

"I hope not too." Tarin scowled and touched his brother's arm. "Maybe we need to swap vehicles again."

"I can't give you Callahan's SUV," Brady argued. "The Jeep should be safe enough."

"I don't mind," Marc said. "We'll swap for now, we can always switch them back again later. Anything to help keep Joy safe is worth it."

Marc Callahan's concern was touching, and it was easy to see the family connection between the Callahans and the Finnegans. Oh, Marc's hair was dark, his eyes green compared to Tarin's red hair and brown eyes, but at their core, they were very much the same.

"Thanks, Marc," Tarin managed a smile. "We appreciate your willingness to help."

"Hey, we're family, right?" Marc teased. "Besides, I'm sure you'd do the same thing if the position was reversed."

"I would," Tarin agreed. Then he playfully elbowed his brother. "Not sure about Brady, though."

"Yeah, yeah." Brady smiled good-naturedly as he held out his hand for Marc's keys.

Tarin gave Brady the keys for the Jeep and accepted Marc's in return. A weird buzzing noise reached her ears, but when she glanced around, she didn't see anything. After everything that happened, her imagination was working overtime. Joy slid into the back seat of Brady's SUV with Tarin as Marc had parked his vehicle farther down the road.

"We'll let you know what we find at Sue's house," Brady said as Tarin and Joy climbed out to get into Marc's vehicle. "Are you sure you don't want a police escort to the motel?"

"I'm sure," Tarin said. "Better for us to go alone, hopefully using Marc's SUV will provide some anonymity."

"Okay, we'll be in touch later, then." Marc flashed a reassuring smile. "Stay safe."

"You too," Tarin said as he opened her door for her. She quickly climbed in so he could do the same.

Swallowing hard, Joy couldn't help feeling vulnerable once the two FBI agents drove away. Not because she didn't trust Tarin, she did. But she sensed there was safety in numbers.

Again, Tarin took a convoluted way to their motel. She was self-conscious of Sue's blood staining her clothes and desperately wished she could change out of them.

But she didn't have anything else to wear, and it was far too dangerous to stop at a store to buy new things. She thought back to the small suitcase she'd taken earlier that day. It was probably still in Aiden's truck, far out of reach.

The thought of her suitcase reminded her of her condo fire and the need to replace most of her wardrobe anyway.

When they finally reached the motel, she rushed inside, heading straight for the bathroom. After soaking a washcloth with cold water, she scrubbed at the stains on her sweater, tears blurring her vision.

Whatever Sue had done, she hadn't deserved to be shot and killed like that. In the middle of the day, no less.

So much death. And for what? Drugs? Money? It was sickening.

The stains wouldn't go away. The tears became sobs until somehow, Tarin was there, drawing her into his arms.

"Shh, it's okay. We're going to get through this. I'll protect you, Joy."

She buried her face against his chest, unable to stop crying. Nothing in her life as an accountant had prepared her for this.

Even if they managed to find and arrest the gunman, her life, like those broken shards of glass, would never be the same.

Never!

HEARING Joy's gulping sobs had ripped at his heart. While he didn't like breaching her privacy, her crying was enough to have him yanking the bathroom door open to reach her.

The way she'd crumpled against him confirmed his fears. Joy had been pushed to the breaking point.

"I'm here," Tarin whispered. He gently led her out of the small bathroom so they could sit on the bed. She wrapped her arm around his waist, holding on tight. "I'm here for you, Joy."

The only response was her tears.

To be fair, he wasn't surprised by her breakdown. She'd faced so much adversity over the past few days. Being a target was one thing, but watching a woman being murdered right in front of your eyes was entirely different.

He wanted to beg her not to cry, but having three sisters had taught him that was the wrong thing to say. Silently supporting them as they cried themselves out was the better option.

Still, it wasn't easy to watch and listen to Joy suffering. He wanted, needed to make her feel better.

Yet all he could give her was his solemn promise that he'd do everything in his power to keep her safe. Frankly, he didn't blame her for not believing in him. So far, she'd been in danger more than anyone he'd ever known.

Well, except for last month when Rhy's fiancée, Devon, had been stalked by a bomber. The situations were very similar, and he could only pray that Joy would survive this the way Devon had.

He couldn't fail her, the way he had Caroline. Not this time. *Please, Lord, not this time!*

Yet they were no closer to uncovering the proof they needed to put an end to the terror. Other than two shell casings, they had squat for leads.

He stroked Joy's back, holding her close and doing his best to soothe her fears. Her sobs slowly quieted, and she sniffled loudly, her face still pressed against her chest.

"The blood—won't wash—away," she said. "I—tried to get—it out."

"Hey, it's okay. I'll get one of my sisters to bring you something to wear." He hesitated, then said, "Quinn or Colin can drop it off somewhere close by. It's better if no one comes all the way to the motel room."

"Are you sure?" She lifted her head from his chest, gazing up at him with puffy, red-rimmed eyes. "I don't want to put anyone in danger. But I hate the thought of having Sue's blood on my clothes . . ."

"It's fine." Tarin offered a reassuring smile. "There is a patch of woods behind the motel. I'm sure we can use that as a drop-off point."

She closed her eyes, reaching up to swipe at her face. "I

can still see the surprise and resignation on her face. Almost as if she knew danger was close by."

"Maybe she did know." Tarin had sympathy for Sue Melius to a point, but if she had known about the drug scheme, she should have reported it to the police, to the feds, to anyone in law enforcement.

He frowned. Unless she had reported it to DEA Agent Doug Bridges. It would explain the recent report Marc had found on the FBI database.

Was he wrong about Bridges being involved? Was it possible the DEA agent was one of the good guys?

Maybe, but he wasn't willing to risk Joy's life by trusting the guy. Or anyone else other than Brady, the rest of his family, and Marc Callahan.

"I'm sorry I got your shirt all wet." She sniffled again, pushing out of his arms long enough to grab the box of tissues nearby. She blew her nose loudly, then came back to sit beside him. "I'm a mess."

"You're beautiful," he said without hesitation. Because it was true. Squashing the urge to kiss her, he added, "Don't apologize, Joy, this has been an incredibly difficult day. I know you've been through a lot."

"So have you." She wiped at her face with another tissue, drying her tears. "I don't know how you do it, Tarin. There's no way I could stand the stress of being in danger every day. I hate thinking about bad guys lurking around every corner."

"This is an extreme situation, Joy." He held her gaze for a long moment. "Even as a cop, I've never been shot at as often as you have over the past two days."

Her gaze was skeptical. "You're just trying to make me feel better. And I appreciate that, truly. But all I can think of is that there's no end in sight. This guy will keep coming after me until I'm dead."

"He's not going to get to you, Joy. Not before we find him." Tarin prayed he was telling her the truth. Hopefully, Brady and Marc would find something useful at Sue Melius's home. "He's taken shots twice now during daylight hours, someone will have seen him. You'd be surprised at how people often come forward after what happened on the news."

"I'm not sure about that." Joy was not convinced. "He's gotten away with everything so far."

He couldn't argue with that, so he changed the subject. "I'll give Elly a call, see when she's finished with class. Elly won't mind loaning out some of her clothes. She's generous that way."

"Your sister is smaller than me," she protested.

"Elly loves oversized sweaters, she'll find something." He wasn't worried about that. The larger issue was getting those items here to the motel.

"Tarin." Joy put a hand on his chest. "I don't know what I'd do without you."

He covered her hand with his. "There isn't anywhere else I'd rather be. Besides, I feel like this is my fault. That if I had been a better detective five years ago, this wouldn't be happening now."

She tipped her head to the side. "I thought you believed in God's plan?"

She had me there. He nodded slowly. "You're right. I do believe in God's plan. Maybe there's a good reason the situation had to unfold in this way." In church, Pastor Stephen would explain that sometimes God put troubles in their path to teach them a lesson or to test their faith.

"I've been praying for our safety since you prayed

before eating that first night," Joy said. "I'm grateful for each day God gives us, but I can't help but wonder how we'll get beyond this. I feel as if the end is inevitable. That maybe God wanted me to come back to my faith before I died."

"Try not to imagine the worst." He tucked a strand of her hair behind her ear, his gaze lingering for a moment on her mouth before he pulled himself back under some semblance of control. He couldn't bear the thought of losing Joy the way he'd lost Caroline. "You're not going to die yet, Joy. Not if I can help it."

"You don't know that," she argued softly. "Only God knows when we'll be called home. The way Jesus was."

"That's exactly right, we are not promised tomorrow, but we can make the most of today, right?" He forced a smile. "Besides, I think the bigger picture here is that we were put into this situation to find this guy and to get him off the street to protect those who are being poisoned with their drugs."

And that, he thought silently, *was something worth fighting for*.

"I agree with you on that point." She stared at him for a long moment, then gave him an impromptu kiss on the cheek. Was it his imagination, or did her lips linger there for a moment? "Thanks for being my rock, Tarin."

"I—uh, of course." He was an idiot to be sidetracked by a casual kiss on the cheek. "It's the least I can do."

"Not true, you're an honorable man, Tarin Finnegan. Most guys I know would cut and run like Kevin did five years ago after I lost Ken." She frowned, then added, "You know, I really thought he'd support me, but instead, he grew annoyed, telling me I was too obsessed with Ken's death not being a suicide. I guess it's true about not knowing someone until you've gone through a difficult time with them. I was shocked when he left me."

"He's an idiot," Tarin said. "Any guy would count his blessings to have you. Besides, now we know your gut instincts were right."

"You say the sweetest things, Tarin."

He was treading on dangerous ground here, but his normal sense of self-preservation seemed to have abandoned him. Why he was so keenly aware of Joy was a mystery as he'd thought his love had died with Caroline.

"Tarin?" She gazed up into his eyes. Then slowly, carefully, she moved her mouth toward his.

He didn't stop her. Just the opposite. He closed the gap, meeting her more than halfway, kissing her the way he'd wanted to for the past hour.

No, longer than an hour. He'd been inexplicably drawn to her since their first meeting.

Kissing Joy was better the second time around, and he would have gladly continued holding her close, but of course, his disposable cell phone rang, interrupting the moment. He ignored the trilling sound until Joy broke off their kiss, laughing softly.

"You'd better get that."

"Do I have to?" He gave her another quick kiss before reaching for the phone. He wasn't surprised to recognize Brady's number. "Hey, bro, tell me you found something good."

"We found a few things, some good, some not so good."

His heart sank, and he held the phone so that Joy could hear the conversation too. "Bad things?"

"Well, for one thing, her personal computer has been wiped clean. And I mean, stripped to its basic operating system."

"You think the gunman knew she had evidence on her computer and destroyed it before getting rid of her?"

"That's the way it looks," Brady agreed. "By our estimation, the deed was done before her death, there wasn't enough time for someone to have done this thorough of a job afterward."

He tried not to sound as dejected as he felt. "Do you think the cybercrime team can rebuild what was on it?"

"Doubtful, according to Marc, but we'll give it a try."

"What's the good news? You must have found something that will help us."

"We did. We found a safe in the corner of her basement. Sue was old-fashioned enough to keep a paper trail. Like literally using paper," Brady clarified. "The gunman must not have realized what she'd stored in that safe, or he didn't bother to look for it. We were able to pry it open."

Tarin sat up straighter. "What did you find?"

"Sue must have secretly run some reports of her own that prove Craig Washington is filling fraudulent scripts. She highlighted the fake ones with a yellow marker. I think maybe she was planning to turn him in at some point." There was a surge of satisfaction in his tone. "We have enough to issue a warrant for his arrest. Marc has already contacted his boss who has also gone to Doug Bridges's boss. We're clear to head over to the pharmacy ASAP."

"Really?" Joy asked, her gaze locked on his.

"Yep. We have a couple of officers stationed at the pharmacy to keep Washington there as we speak. We're heading over to take him into custody. I'll be in touch later, okay?"

"Thanks, Brady." Tarin lowered the phone as Joy threw herself in his arms.

"It's over," she whispered.

"It will be," he promised. The danger wouldn't be

completely over until Craig confessed to his crimes and gave up the identity of the shooter.

But they were one step closer than they had been an hour ago. Holding Joy, he hoped and prayed the danger would soon end.

CHAPTER THIRTEEN

They were going to arrest Craig Washington! Hope filled Joy's heart that maybe her brother would get the justice he deserved.

And that she could finally get back to routine and boring life.

"Interesting that Sue Melius was keeping records," Tarin said thoughtfully. "I wonder if she was cooperating with Bridges all along."

"Not all along or Craig would have been arrested by now, don't you think?" Joy rested her head against Tarin's shoulder. For the first time in what seemed like forever, she relaxed.

"Maybe not for the past five years, but the past few months? Oh yeah, that's possible. Especially if she discovered Leon had been killed. It's possible she wasn't buying the coincidence of both Leon and your brother dying so unexpectedly."

"Still, Leon has been gone a while." She hated knowing that two men had lost their lives over this. "The good news is that this nightmare is over."

"We're not leaving the motel yet," Tarin cautioned.

She straightened to look at him. "Once Craig Washington is behind bars, I'm sure the gunman will disappear, knowing his job of killing me is no longer needed."

"That's our hope, but we don't know when the gunman will get the news of Washington's arrest." Tarin smiled encouragingly. "But soon, Joy. I really think Washington will start talking to get a lighter sentence. I'm sure he'll realize there's no point in lying once he sees the evidence. We should be able to get out of here very soon."

"I hope so." Looking up at Tarin, she a pang of regret hit hard. She'd miss him. After spending the last two days with him, she silently admitted there was no other man she admired more.

He had her heart, even though he didn't want it.

"Let's turn on the news. I'm sure this arrest will get some coverage, especially due to the location of the pharmacy to the café shooting." Tarin eased away, reaching for the remote.

She missed his warmth and tried to ignore her damp sweater, still stained with Sue's blood. Despite knowing she was safe here with Tarin, the memory of Sue's last moments haunted her.

Learning now how the tech had kept key documents in her safe, it was easy to see why there had been a flash of resignation in the woman's gaze as she'd been shot and killed. As if she'd known the dangerous game she'd been playing.

If only she and Tarin had tried to talk to Sue sooner. Showing up at the pharmacy may have been a mistake, and she prayed their visit hadn't put Sue in the crosshairs. She sincerely hoped Sue had been trying to do the right thing by going to the DEA.

"We can probably trust Doug Bridges, don't you think?" She watched at Tarin flipped through the channels searching for a news station. "I'm sure he got his information from Sue Melius."

"He may have." He glanced at her. "But I'm not ready to lower my guard yet. Not until Washington is arrested and starts talking."

And how long would that take? She suppressed a sigh. Now that the end of this nightmare was so close, it was even harder to sit back and be patient.

Tarin stopped on a news channel where a crew was stationed outside the café where Sue had died. Her stomach churned while listening to the anchor woman recap the event she'd lived firsthand.

"We are live outside the Baker's Best Café," the anchor woman said. "I've spoken to three witnesses who heard the gunfire. However, we have not been given any more information other than there has been one female victim declared deceased at the scene."

The camera went back to the studio, where another anchor man asked, "When will we learn the identity of the victim or a possible motive for the shooting?"

"That's a good question, Tim, I don't know that information yet." The woman abruptly turned to look behind her. "Tim, it looks as if there is something going on at the Craig's Corner Pharmacy across the street."

The camera zoomed in on a familiar black SUV pulling up to the front door. Joy's eyes widened as she saw Brady and Marc emerge from the vehicle and walk inside.

"They're going to capture his arrest on television," she whispered, hardly able to believe what she was watching. This moment was so long in coming, she found herself holding her breath while waiting for the FBI agents return.

"I've been told there are officers stationed at the pharmacy too," the anchor woman continued. "But it's still unclear as to what is happening."

Brady stepped out the door first, leading a cuffed Craig Washington toward the vehicle. Behind Craig, Marc stood, his expression grim. The anchorwoman continued to give a running commentary on what could be clearly seen on the video, but Joy tuned her out.

Craig was in custody, and that was the most important thing. She knew more than the anchorwoman did about why Craig had been arrested.

She released her pent-up breath, watching as the SUV backed out of the pharmacy parking lot and disappeared down the road. "I'm sure the pharmacy will close now that he's been taken into custody."

"I hope so, but that depends on whether or not the judge grants bail." Tarin shrugged. "I'm hoping the federal prosecutor will make it clear that lives are at risk if Washington is released and allowed to work."

She hadn't considered the fact that Craig may be released on bail. "The evidence will surely prevent that."

"I think so." Tarin smiled. "Try not to stress. From what Brady tells me, the federal prosecutors are tougher than the locals when it comes to being charged with dispensing illegal narcotics."

"Okay, I won't stress." Her smile faded as she glanced down at her stained sweater again. "I'm just sorry Sue had to die for the truth about Craig to come out."

"I know." Tarin must have noticed her obsession with the blood stains on her sweater because he quickly out his phone. "Let me call Elly the way I promised. I know she'll pull something together for you."

"Thanks, but I'll be fine," she protested.

"You need something clean to wear," he said firmly. "And I don't plan on letting Elly come here, even with Craig's arrest. One of my brothers will drive it over."

She nodded, secretly relieved at the possibility to have clean clothes. She watched as Tarin stood and moved through the connecting doorway to make his call.

The news anchor was still talking about the arrest at the pharmacy, keenly speculating that it was connected to the shooting at the café. She turned the volume down so she didn't have to listen.

The shooting had left her badly shaken, reliving those moments with the help of the anchorwoman was not helping. She wondered if she'd ever get over Sue's murder. Losing Ken had been hard, but he hadn't died right in front of her.

She closed her eyes and prayed that God would allow Sue to rest in peace and that He would continue to watch over Brady, Marc, and Tarin as they sought justice. Lastly, she prayed that Craig would repent his sins and tell the FBI and the DEA everything he knew about the drug scheme.

She wanted desperately to go home. Too bad, she didn't have a home. She didn't even have a car, hers was still at the shop.

Tarin returned a few minutes later. "Elly just got home from her class, she's rummaging through her closet for clothes. Nothing fancy," he cautioned. "Mostly yoga pants and sweatshirts."

"Sounds wonderful." She wasn't about to complain. Stretchy clothes would have a better chance of fitting her anyway.

"Quinn is going to drop them off in about an hour. I've asked him to pick up lunch, too, since we didn't get a chance to eat." Tarin searched her gaze. "I hope that's okay with you."

"Of course." She wasn't the least bit hungry, but maybe once she had clean clothes to wear, she'd feel better. "That's nice of him to take time from his schedule for us."

"He's off for the next few weeks, his job for the Coast Guard working on Lake Michigan keeps him busy, but in the winter, they have less rescues and drug-trafficking arrests to manage. They spend more time helping to break up ice for cargo ships to pass by. Along with the occasional ice rescue."

She'd never personally known anyone in the Coast Guard but wasn't surprised to find one of the Finnegans had chosen to work for the military. It certainly seemed as if they'd all taken jobs that held an element of danger. "Well, it's still nice of him to come."

Tarin dropped down beside her. "Once you can change and eat something, you might consider getting some rest."

"I'm not sure that's possible." She instantly regretted her dejected tone and added, "But I'll do my best. I know all we can do now is wait to learn from Craig who else is involved in this."

"True. Patience is not my best trait," Tarin confessed with a teasing gaze. "But as an accountant, I'd think that is right up your alley."

"Usually, it's not a problem." She glanced around the small motel room. "Then again, I'm not normally in a place like this without the ability to focus on work."

Tarin snapped his fingers and picked up his phone. "Good point, I'll ask Quinn to bring my computer too. I think it's at the homestead."

The way he eagerly went out of his way to make her happy was touching. And honestly, something she'd never experienced before, except from her brother. Being with Tarin only highlighted, with bright neon flashing lights, the problems she'd had with Kevin. Now it was easy to see how God's plan had been correct all along. It was good that Kevin had broken things off, even if he couldn't have picked a worse time.

She was better off without him. Without a man in general, unless he was someone like Tarin.

The next thirty minutes passed slowly with nothing to do except watch television. Tarin glanced at his watch frequently until finally his phone rang. "Quinn, is that you?"

She couldn't hear his brother's side of the conversation but could tell they were making arrangements to meet up in the woods behind the motel.

"Is that really necessary?" she asked when he'd finished his call. "Now that Craig has been arrested, I'm not sure why he couldn't come to the door."

"I asked Quinn to make sure he isn't followed, but he's not a cop. I guess I'd rather meet in a neutral place away from prying eyes. Quinn is going to park down the street and come through the back on foot."

"Okay." What did she know about clandestine operations? Only what little she'd seen on television.

"Don't worry. I'll be back soon." Tarin gave her a quick hug.

She wanted to cling to him but forced herself to release him. "Thanks again, Tarin."

He nodded and slipped out through the motel room door. She watched him for a moment, but he simply walked along the front of the motel toward the lobby. Likely, he'd wait until the return trip to grab the computer case.

Turning away from the window, she pulled out her

disposable phone. Maybe she should call her boss and let him know she'll be returning to work. Maybe he'd have a job she could do remotely, here from the motel.

She heard the sound of a key being used on her door. Maybe Tarin had forgotten something. She pocketed her phone and went over to meet him.

But the man who stood there wasn't Tarin. It was her former boyfriend, Kevin Creek. He smirked at her. "Hello, Joy."

She froze, ice congealing in her veins when she saw he had a gun leveled at her chest.

TARIN HOPED he wasn't making a mistake in leaving Joy alone for a few minutes. Meeting Quinn in the woods behind the motel seemed like overkill, but he couldn't discount the possibility that Craig had someone watching the Finnegan homestead and might follow Quinn to their location.

Best to keep some distance between their meetup and Joy's motel room.

The news of Washington's arrest should have reached the gunman by now. But he also knew the guy might be waiting to see if the pharmacist would be released on bail. The wheels of justice often moved slowly. If Washington was granted bail and demanded a trial, it would likely take a full year for the case to go to court. By then they'd have plenty of time to eliminate evidence.

The way they'd callously eliminated witnesses.

He stepped into the lobby, then asked to see the rear exit. All buildings had them since they were required by fire code.

The clerk curiously eyed his badge, then showed him the way. At the door, Tarin paused. "I need this to remain unlocked so I can come back in this way."

The clerk frowned. "We don't allow people to come in this way."

Tarin drilled him with an intent gaze. "Make an exception. I won't be long, and you can lock it back up when I return."

With a reluctant nod of agreement, the clerk removed a key ring and unlocked the door.

"Thanks," Tarin said. "Appreciate the cooperation." Without waiting for a response, he slipped outside. Pausing, he glanced around for a moment to make sure there was no one around. The area appeared deserted, so he darted into the woods, using the large, wide evergreen trees for cover. The snow had melted in some areas, so he lengthened his stride, stepping in those openings to avoid leaving a visible trail.

He paused behind a large oak tree, searching for signs of Quinn. Glancing at his watch, he realized he was a little early. The chill in the air wasn't as cold as the day before, but spring was a long way from now.

After a long five minutes, he saw movement between the trees ahead of him. He straightened when he caught sight of Quinn's blond hair as he moved through the woods toward him.

"I got everything you asked for," his brother said as they met in the middle of the woods. "By the way, Aiden's truck is back home where he'll never have to know that you used it as a race car."

Tarin winced. "Yeah, the less Aiden knows, the better."

"Oh, and here is a duffel bag of clothes and toiletries Elly sent along."

"No lunch?" Tarin asked, disappointed.

"Lunch is in a bag inside the duffel." Quinn grinned. "I thought about letting you starve but figured that wouldn't be fair to Joy."

"Thanks," Tarin said dryly. "We appreciate you feeding us."

"I saw the news about Washington's arrest," Quinn said.

Tarin nodded as he slung the duffel and computer bag over his shoulder. "Yeah, the sooner he talks, the better off Joy will be. I'm worried the gunman will keep coming after her unless Washington gives up his identity."

"That may not happen for a while," Quinn said with a frown. "Are you planning to stay at the motel indefinitely?"

"For now, yes." Tarin didn't see that there was another option. The duffel was unusually heavy. "What did you bring us to eat, bricks?"

Quinn chuckled. "No, but Elly packed some things for you too. I guess she wanted to be sure you were both comfortable."

"That was sweet of her," Tarin said. The youngest Finnegan had the softest heart. "Tell her thanks, will you?"

"Sure." Quinn held his gaze for a long moment. "The younger siblings are worried about you, Tarin. We just went through this with Rhy and Devon."

"My situation isn't anything like that," he protested, although it kinda was. "Rhy brought Devon to the homestead. I've been doing my best to keep Joy away from the others so they aren't in danger."

"Yeah, but Elly thinks you and Joy would be safer at the house with a security system than staying in two-star motels. Frankly, I agree with her." Quinn grimaced. "I wasn't around when Rhy was protecting Devon, but I'm here now. If this goes on much longer, you should reconsider your strategy. I'm happy to move back to the homestead temporarily if that helps add a level of safety."

"Thanks, Quinn, that's good to know." He thought about it for a moment. His brother had a point about the timeline dragging on. He wouldn't be allowed to take off much more time from work.

And he trusted his brothers Aiden and Quinn to keep Joy and their sisters safe. Both men were armed and dangerous. It would be difficult for anyone to get past them.

"Okay." He slowly nodded. "Brady and Marc Callahan just took Washington into custody. I'm hoping to hear from Brady very soon, especially if he gets a lead on the gunman." He clapped Quinn on the back. "Thanks for the offer. I may take you up on that."

"I'm here for you," Quinn assured him. "I wish I could have been there to help Rhy and Devon too."

"Rhy doesn't blame you for working," Tarin pointed out. "It was hairy there for a while, but it ended well, didn't it?"

"Rhy absolutely deserves to be happy," Quinn agreed. "Devon is good for him."

"True." For some reason, that made him think of Joy. He gave himself a mental shake. "Thanks again for bringing the supplies. I need to get back, but I'll keep in touch if my plans change anytime soon."

"Understood. I'll leave you to it." Quinn flashed another smile, then turned to leave the same way he'd come.

Tarin did the same. Through the trees, he could just barely make out the back of the motel. Moving quietly through the woods wasn't as easy while carrying two bags, they brushed with what seemed like excruciating loudness against the evergreen branches. The area still looked deserted, though, so he pushed forward, retracing his steps.

If he were honest, the growling of his stomach, along with the promise of lunch, made him want to hurry. When he reached the back door, he pulled it open and eased inside.

Taking the short hallway, he entered the lobby. There was someone at the front desk speaking to the clerk about a room. He was about to leave, but a stab of guilt nagged at him.

He stood, waiting to snag the clerk's attention. He'd promised the guy he could lock up when he was finished, and a Finnegan always kept a promise.

A full minute ticked by before the man moved away. The desk clerk looked up and then nodded when Tarin waved at him.

"I'm finished," he called out. "Thanks."

"No problem." The clerk hurried out from behind the desk, pulling his keys out to relock the door.

Tarin was impressed the guy took his job seriously and wondered how Brady managed to convince him to take cash for their room. He shrugged it off, heading out the main lobby door and walking down the sidewalk to his and Joy's adjoining rooms.

He had to skirt the housekeeping cart as he did so, making a mental note to put the do not disturb sign out so that the housekeeper wouldn't bother them. The last thing he wanted was a stranger working in either of their rooms.

Tarin's room was before Joy's, so he stopped there and used his key card to get inside. He pushed the door open and immediately crossed over to set the computer bag and duffel on the bed.

"Joy?" He didn't hear any sound coming from her room. She was probably in the bathroom, so he opened the duffel, removed the fast-food bag, and carried it through the connecting door to set up their lunch on the table.

The silence was absolute. The tiny hairs rose on the back of his neck as he quickly went to check the bathroom.

It was empty.

"Joy?" He scanned the room, then hurried over to check his on the off chance she'd decided to use his bathroom. But that was empty too.

Something was wrong. No way would Joy disappear without a word. He didn't know how, but the gunman must have found her.

He grabbed his phone and called Quinn. "Joy is missing. I need you to turn around and come back to the motel."

"Will do," Quinn agreed.

Panic seized him by the throat. He'd only been gone eighteen minutes! How could this have happened? He had no clue but forced himself to think like a cop, to examine the motel room for clues.

It was rare that people disappeared without a trace.

But there was no sign of a struggle. No secret note left behind to give him an idea of where to find her. Her phone wasn't there either, which didn't mean much. The gunman could have taken it from her, rendering the device useless.

The complete lack of evidence, the hollow emptiness of the room, was like a punch to his gut.

The only explanation he could come up with was that she'd been taken at gunpoint. Joy would have put up a fight if she was able.

Lord, help me! Show me the way! Keep Joy safe in Your care until I can find her!

The prayer did little to ease his concerns. A tsunami of guilt hit hard. He never should have left her alone, not for a minute!

Only the sound of a car engine helped keep him upright. He flung open the door in time to see Quinn jumping out of an SUV. "What happened?"

"I don't know." Tarin had never felt so helpless in his entire life. "I don't understand how, but the gunman must have discovered this location and made his move the minute I left her alone."

"Okay, blaming yourself isn't helpful," Quinn said, a look of concern darkening his eyes. "Who was next in line on your suspect list?"

Tarin reached for his phone again. "I haven't spoken to my partner, Dave, but I am wondering if the arrest by Brady and Marc caused DEA Agent Doug Bridges to do this. Maybe he thinks Joy knows more than she does."

"Are you calling Brady?" Quinn asked.

"Yes." He almost wept in relief when his brother answered. "Brady, Joy's missing, the gunman has her. I need to know where Doug Bridges is."

"He's here with us. He claims Sue Melius was working as his informant."

"Any chance he made a call to someone? Telling them to get Joy?"

"He hasn't touched his phone since we've been here." Brady's voice held concern. "I don't understand how the gunman found her."

"I need help finding her." There was no hiding the desperation in his voice. "You need to lean hard on Craig Washington, force him to tell you who else is involved."

"I will. I'll call as soon as I learn anything." Brady disconnected from the call.

Tarin stared down at his phone wondering if it would make Joy's situation worse if he tried to call her. As if reading his thoughts, Joy's number flashed on the screen.

He tentatively lifted the phone to his ear. Some instinct made him wait for her to say something.

"I don't understand why you're doing this, Kevin. Craig has already been arrested. Why bother to kill me?"

Kevin? The memory of Joy's former boyfriend flashed in his mind. Putting the phone against his chest, he whispered to Quinn. "Call Brady, tell him Kevin Creek has Joy."

Quinn nodded and moved into the next room to make the call. Tarin lifted the phone back to his ear, praying Joy would be able to give him additional information to find her.

CHAPTER FOURTEEN

Joy did everything possible to keep Kevin talking while having her cell phone in her pocket. It was the only advantage she had considering he'd bound her wrists together and stuck her in the back seat of the dark sedan. If her ex-boyfriend found the device, she didn't doubt he'd kill her on the spot.

Frankly, she was surprised he hadn't just shot her already, but apparently after missing all the previous attempts, he'd decided to take her someplace secluded to do the deed. She had to assume he'd try to hide her body for as long as possible too.

"You realize Craig Washington is in federal custody, right?" She wet her dry lips. "What's the point of killing me now? I'm sure Craig will talk to save his own skin. There's no reason to add murder to the list."

"One murder or two, what's the difference?" Kevin's callously snide tone sent a wave of nausea washing over her. "Besides, I'm not working for Washington."

"You're not?" She prayed Tarin could hear this conversation even with the cheap phone tucked in her jacket pocket. "Who, then? Dr. Eli Lewis is in jail, I know another doc has taken over his business, or Craig wouldn't be able to keep filling the prescriptions. Which doc are you working for?"

"I never said I was working for anyone," Kevin said coldly. "If you just would have kept your mouth shut, you wouldn't be sitting here now."

"I haven't spoken to you in years." Somehow, she knew logic wouldn't work, so she switched gears. "How did you know about my plan to talk to Detective Finnegan?" She tried not to sound as panicked as she felt. "Did you bug my phone?"

"My tech skills are wasted at the hospital," he bragged. "I was able to watch what you did on your phone and your computer. When I noticed you were spending a lot of time researching Eli Lewis, I knew you were going to request the cops reopen your brother's case."

Her phone and her computer? She swallowed hard, horrified by the way he'd breached her privacy. And for five full years!

That seemed extreme, even for Kevin.

"W-why would you care if I asked Ta—er, Detective Finnegan to reopen the case? You do realize he initially turned me down, don't you? You must have heard my conversation with him if you bugged my phone."

"I heard," Kevin said. "He believed you."

Had he? So much had happened since then, she barely remembered their first interaction. "That doesn't mean his boss would have agreed to look into Ken's death. If you hadn't started shooting at me, he might not have bothered."

"We knew someone was talking to the feds." Kevin scowled. "I thought it was you at first, especially when you searched on Eli Lewis and then found Finnegan."

"I wasn't," she said.

"Yeah, well, we didn't realize that it was that useless woman Washington had working for him until recently. Stupid idiot should have known better than to trust her for so long. She needed to be silenced."

She stared at him in horror. "It was you! You shot Sue in the back before she could talk to me."

He met her gaze briefly, and she imagined she saw a flicker of satisfaction in his eyes. "Not that the little bit the feds know really matters in the long run," he went on as if she hadn't spoken.

"Why not?" she forced herself to ask.

"Do you really think Washington's pharmacy is the only game in town?" Kevin's evil smile made her shiver as she hated to acknowledge he was too smart to admit to being a cold-blooded murderer.

Even here, in the privacy of his vehicle.

Then his words sank in. Not the only game in town. Swallowing hard, she realized their investigation had been too narrowly focused. Of course, Craig's Corner wasn't the only pharmacy filling those fraudulent prescriptions. She and Tarin knew there were others, but there hadn't been time to investigate further. Her brother working for Craig was the only solid lead they'd had.

"How many others are involved?" She pushed the question through her tight throat.

"Enough that we'll survive this little bump in the road."

Bump in the road? He saw murdering her as little more than an inconvenience. His vague and threatening responses were messing with her head. "If you're not worried, then why am I here, Kevin? Seriously, I really want to know. What do you have to gain? Why are you still so intent on killing me?"

"I knew you'd figure out I was involved eventually." He shrugged. "Better to shut you down than to take the risk."

"I didn't know you were involved!" she shouted, losing her patience. "And if you had a bug in my phone and my computer, you knew that! I was no threat to you, not until you started shooting at me!"

"Ah, but you ditched your phone and your computer." He was eerily calm, although when his gaze met hers in the rearview mirror, she could see dark anger simmering there. "And that concerned me. I figured you'd found the bugs, which forced my hand. I needed to go to other extremes to find you."

"You burned my house."

He shrugged, but the creepy grin on his face confirmed her suspicions. No wonder he'd started the fire in her bed. It was a personal slap because she'd refused to sleep with him.

She swallowed hard. "And you must have had Craig's pharmacy staked out or you wouldn't have known I was in the Baker's Best Café." She had to admit she wouldn't have given Kevin the credit of being smart enough to do all of this. "And when you knew Sue was coming inside and might talk to me, you shot her."

"I'm good." His tone was matter of fact. His arrogance was unbelievable. She wanted to punch him but knew that even if her wrists weren't bound together, she wasn't strong enough to take him on.

She was an accountant who had never stepped foot in a gym. Tears pricked her eyes as she realized how easy she'd made this for him. He must have gotten the key from the motel maid. Then he'd bound her wrists, taken her from the motel, and would soon kill her.

And there was nothing she could do to stop him.

"So now what?" Her flash of anger faded into resignation. Even with Tarin listening in, he'd never reach her in time. "Where are you taking me?"

"Someplace you can disappear without anyone being the wiser."

Tears pricked her eyes as she turned to stare out the window. She wasn't dead yet, there was still time for her to attempt to escape. But with her wrists zip-tied together, and being in the back seat where he had the child protection locks engaged, she'd have to wait until they reached their destination.

Wherever it was.

One thing she knew, they were heading east. Her analytical mind tended to use proper directions rather than landmarks, which often changed. But to be fair, it was also easy for those living in Milwaukee to keep track of which direction was which as Lake Michigan was always east. "I hope you're not planning to toss me into Lake Michigan. That may be difficult as it's all iced over, especially close to shore."

Kevin didn't respond. She was afraid to say too much in case she raised his suspicions.

Staring down at her hands, she carefully eased her wrists to the right toward her jacket pocket. Using the phone to connect with Tarin had seemed like a good idea once she was in the back seat, but now she couldn't help wondering if the connection had been lost. It wasn't as if their phones were expensive smartphones. Quite the opposite.

Keeping her gaze on the window, she slipped the phone out just enough that she could glance down to confirm the line was still connected.

Pushing the phone back into her pocket, she bowed her

head and closed her eyes. *Thank You, Lord! Keep me safe! Guide Tarin and his brothers so they can find me!*

The silent prayer helped calm her nerves. Even if she didn't survive to live another day, she knew God was watching over her. And that she'd be home with Him after Kevin completed his task of killing her.

"May God's will be done. Amen." She didn't realize she'd said the words out loud until Kevin responded.

"You're praying now?" He snorted. "Too late, Joy. God can't save you now."

"You're wrong." She lifted her chin, meeting his gaze defiantly. "God sent Jesus to save me. I'm not afraid of you, Kevin, or what you plan to do to me. We are all going to die, but the difference is that when my turn comes, I'll be with my Lord God."

A flicker of uncertainty darkened his eyes, but then he smirked. "Good one. You keep telling yourself that."

"I plan to." She didn't back down. She lifted her gaze up and continued praying out loud. "Dear Lord, please save me from this evil man's plans as he is not a believer. He knows what he's doing in wrong in Your eyes, Lord. He is intentionally breaking Your commandments. Save me or bring me home to You, in Jesus's name. Amen."

"Knock it off," Kevin growled. "I don't want to hear anything more from you."

She was tempted to ignore him, but again, she didn't want to force his hand too early. She clung to the faint hope that Tarin and his brothers might be able to find her in time. Or at least find Kevin and arrest him, even if it was too late to save her.

It was disheartening to know how many more illegal drugs would continue to make their way into the public's hands if they didn't arrest Kevin and the others involved.

She reminded herself that no matter what happened in the next hour, Tarin, Brady, Marc, and the others would not rest until they'd broken up the entire fraudulent prescription ring.

She caught a glimpse of a passing street sign. "I thought you'd be smarter than taking me to the south shore of the lakefront." She prayed Tarin was listening. "I thought we already established you can't toss my body into the lake this time of year."

"Shut up!" For the first time, she saw a crack in her ex-boyfriend's tough outer shell. He wasn't nearly as immune to her praying or her derisive comments as he pretended to be. She was human enough to feel a flash of satisfaction at getting under his skin.

A renewed sense of determination filled her with steely resolve.

Maybe she wasn't physically strong, but she was smart. Kevin was arrogant enough and maybe desperate enough to make a mistake.

And when he did, she intended to catch him off guard and capitalize on it. With God's strength and guidance, anything was possible.

LISTENING to Joy's conversation with Kevin Creek was torture. Even with her comments about the lakefront, the shoreline occupied many miles. Without more details, they would never know where she was.

Yet that didn't prevent him from relaying every bit of intel he'd learned from the conversation to Brady. Including the bit about how there were multiple other pharmacies involved.

"I need something on Creek," Tarin said now. "We have to find him!"

"He's driving a black sedan with the following license plate, TKY 1602," Brady said in his ear. He had to add an earpiece so that he could hear both his brother Brady, who was at the FBI offices, and Quinn, who was driving while listening to Joy's open phone line at the same time. Thankfully, he'd been able to mute the disposable phone so that his three-way conversation with Quinn and Brady couldn't be heard by Joy's assailant.

Quinn asked, "Is there a police or FBI chopper in the air?"

"Working on it," Brady replied.

Quinn scowled, and Tarin knew that as a member of the Coast Guard, he'd have preferred to be up in the air ready to jump down to rescue Joy. Especially after her comment about being tossed into the water. Quinn had always been the more adventurous one of the family, taking his first skydiving lessons before their parents had died when he was nineteen. It was right after that, that he'd joined the Coast Guard.

The rescue would be near impossible, especially since there was ice along the shores of Lake Michigan. Quinn had verbalized his agreement in her assessment, yet he felt certain Kevin had a plan to make her disappear beneath the water.

Maybe Kevin knew of a place where the ice wasn't as thick and planned to make it look as if Joy accidentally fell through. With the water at freezing temperatures, he didn't doubt she'd die quickly of hypothermia.

Tarin tried not to panic at the unlimited ways Kevin Creek could kill Joy. The worst-case scenario was that Creek could simply shoot her, dump her body someplace close by, and disappear before they could stop him.

He silently thanked God for keeping her safe this far and prayed that he and his brothers would reach her in time. It was difficult to remain calm, but he used every ounce of his thirteen years of police training to do just that.

"We just received permission to send up a chopper," Brady said. "But it's going to take a few minutes to get the team airborne."

"She may not have a few minutes." Tarin hated feeling so helpless. "He can shoot her at any second."

"You still have the phone connection open and working, don't you?" Brady asked. "That should help us find her if she continues to provide clues as to her location."

"Yes." He pulled out the disposable phone and double-checked that the line was still active. The phones were cheap, but so far, they'd done their job.

It was quiet on Joy's end of the phone, which concerned him. Then he noticed the tiny battery icon, and his heart sank. "My phone only has fifteen percent of its battery left. I have no way of knowing if Joy's is the same or lower than that." The thought of losing the only tangible connection he had filled him with dread.

There was a long silence from Brady. "We're going to find her, Tarin. Just keep heading toward the south shore. I'll let you know when the chopper is up."

"Make it happen faster, Brady," Quinn said, his voice mirroring Tarin's concern. "They may already be at the south shore. We're still three minutes out."

"I'm doing my best," Brady said.

It was on the tip of his tongue to lash back, saying that Brady's best wasn't good enough, but he managed to hold back. Everyone was doing what they could to find Kevin Creek.

Tarin knew that this situation was his fault. He should have ignored her request for clean clothes. He'd been lulled into a sense of complacency after learning Washington had been arrested.

He'd failed Joy by allowing her to get too close. And now she may die because of his error in judgment.

Was this how Rhy had felt when Devon had been missing? He understood his brother's rash actions better now. Because even though he'd known better than to get emotionally involved with Joy, he'd gone ahead and done it anyway.

He'd fallen in love with her.

As if sensing his despair, Quinn hit the gas, weaving in and out of traffic, ignoring the blaring horns of annoyance reverberating in their wake. There was still no sign of the chopper overhead, which only added to his anxiety. They had to find Joy, they just had to!

When Tarin saw the sign indicating they were nearing the south shore, he scanned the area for the black sedan. He touched his earpiece. "Brady, was the black sedan an electric car of some sort? There was one that moved past Joy's house that was completely silent, we never heard it until after shots were fired."

"Yeah, it's not a Tesla, but it's a similar model put out by another car manufacturer," Brady said. "That may work to our advantage, maybe he'll run out of power."

Tarin didn't agree. "More likely he'll slip behind some buildings or something, and we won't know he's there until it's too late."

"Have faith, Tarin," Brady said. "The chopper will be able to find him."

Tarin wanted to believe him, but it was difficult to maintain his composure. He wanted to lash out in anger but knew that was counterproductive. He needed to think, to stay sharp. They weren't that far behind them.

He continued searching for signs of a black sedan that didn't have an exhaust pipe sticking out of the back end. It wasn't easy, but soon the traffic thinned out a bit, which helped. People didn't go down to Lake Michigan much in the cold winter months.

"Why are we stopping?" Joy's voice jarred him from his search. She'd been silent for so long he'd worried Kevin may have slapped duct tape over her mouth to shut her up. Listening to their exchange, it had been obvious Joy's prayers had knocked Creek off-balance.

"I told you to shut up!" Creek's sharp voice made Tarin curl his fingers into fists.

"What's the point? You're just going to shoot me anyway."

This was the second time she'd mentioned the gun. Tarin appreciated her warning, but at the same time, he wanted to beg her to cooperate with Creek, stalling for as long as possible. She had no way of knowing they were following them, but he silently willed her to stay strong.

Joy was smarter than Creek by a long shot.

The sound of a car door opening and closing sent a chill down his spine. "Brady, we need that chopper up! They're stopped and getting out of the vehicle!"

"The bird is going up right now," Brady replied.

"From which location?" Quinn asked.

"Timmerman," Brady responded.

Tarin caught Quinn's concerned gaze, hanging on to his patience by a thread. "That's north of where we need it to be."

"In five minutes, maybe less, they'll be over the south

shore," Brady said confidently. "Do you have eyes on the black sedan?"

"Not yet." Quinn scowled as he slowed their vehicle. He turned onto Lake Front Drive and headed south.

"The parking lot in front of the south shore marina is up ahead." Tarin frowned too. "But it looks empty."

"Go there anyway, maybe he's parked in a corner someplace," Brady said. "You'll be glad to know Washington's lawyer said he's willing to talk."

"Yeah, great. Hours too late," Tarin snapped. "If he'd cooperated from the beginning, we'd have Creek in custody too."

"We're learning about three more pharmacies," Brady said, ignoring his short-tempered response. "And we have a lead on the doc who took over for Eli Lewis."

All of that was good news for the investigation, but Tarin didn't care. Not at this moment anyway. Rescuing Joy from Creek was the only thing that mattered.

He was seriously concerned they'd find her too late.

"I think there's a car up ahead," Quinn said, interrupting his dire thoughts. "I caught a glimpse of the sun glinting off what might be a windshield."

His pulse quickened. "Where?"

"Look at the area southeast of us behind the marina. I don't think there's any parking on that side of the building, but he probably drove there anyway." Quinn slowed the car's pace, then abruptly pulled over and stopped, quickly killing the engine. His voice dropped. "It might be better for us to go on foot from here."

"Okay." He pushed open his passenger-side door and stepped out into the frigid air. The wind blowing over the icy lake always ensured it was colder here compared to the inland suburbs. From what little he could see beyond the building, there were no boats in the water and that made sense as there was clearly nothing but ice along the shoreline.

No soothing sounds of the waves lapping at the shore, that was for sure.

"Ready?" Quinn asked in a whisper. He was thankful his brother Quinn had brought his service weapon along. He pulled his 9mm and nodded.

Together, they lightly ran across the open parking lot toward the closed marina. The structure was located between them and the lakeshore. Tarin tried to remember what was on the other side, but his mind was a blank. He didn't normally come to this section of the lakefront. Quinn had mentioned no parking was allowed there, but there had to be a walkway leading to the water.

When they reached the building, Tarin motioned for Quinn to go one way to approach the building from the south while he headed north. "Meet you on the other side," Tarin whispered.

Quinn nodded, and they split up. Unfortunately, their dark clothing was more visible than he'd have liked against the white building.

But that couldn't be helped.

There was no sign of the chopper yet, which was frustrating. When Tarin reached the corner, he paused, took a deep breath, then risked a quick glance.

No one was there. And from here, he couldn't see the black sedan either.

Easing around the corner, he inched along the north wall. As he stepped closer, he heard voices.

"Here?" Joy said, her tone incredulous. "You've got to be joking."

"Shut up!" Kevin repeated.

No! Tarin silently shouted, imagining Kevin had set her up against the wall to kill her, execution style. He swiftly reached the next corner and peeked around it.

Joy wasn't up against the wall, but she was standing just beyond the rear passenger door with her wrists bound together. She stood still, but he thought she glanced toward the icy lakefront.

Kevin Creek stood less than six feet away, his gun trained on her.

From his position, he couldn't take a shot at Creek without the guy shooting Joy. The vehicle was partially in the way, and Joy was too close for comfort. It was a stalemate of the worst kind.

Any second, Creek might simply shoot her and be done with it.

Although he had many chances to do so without succeeding. Was it possible the guy couldn't pull the trigger while looking her in the face? It may explain why he'd taken so many shots at her from a distance.

Easier to shoot a person if you couldn't see their eyes.

Tarin tried to think of a way to distract Creek's attention. A diversion would be nice, but he didn't see anything nearby.

Except for himself. Tarin took a deep breath and decided he'd use himself as a diversion. Maybe he'd get the guy to shoot at him, giving Quinn the chance to take him down from the opposite direction.

Before he could move, though, the sound of a chopper reached his ears. Tarin noticed Creek's gaze lift to the sky and made his move.

He jumped out from behind the building. "Police! Put your hands up!"

At the exact same moment, Joy sprinted away from the

vehicle, running directly toward the snow-covered icy lakefront. He wasn't sure why she'd gone that way, other than there weren't many options, but her abrupt decision to run helped cause additional confusion.

Everything seemed to happen in slow motion, much like the day he'd lost Caroline. Creek's gaze darted toward Tarin before he turned his weapon toward Joy.

Gunfire reverberated through the air, but it only took a few seconds for Tarin to realize Creek was hit. The man collapsed to the ground, his gun dropping to the ground beside him. When he saw Quinn standing behind Creek's prone body, he gave his brother a nod.

"Joy!" Tarin sprinted after her. "It's okay! Kevin's dead!"

She abruptly stopped, turning to face him. "He is?"

"Yes." He kept rushing toward her until he heard a cracking sound. That was when he realized she was standing on the ice. "Be careful!"

More cracking sounds made his heart thunder in his chest. He weighed more than she did, so he didn't dare move any closer.

He didn't want Joy to fall through the ice, losing her forever.

CHAPTER FIFTEEN

"Joy, you need to distribute your weight," Quinn said, hurrying over to join Tarin. The chopper she'd heard earlier was louder now as it hovered overhead. Quinn waved his arms, indicating it needed to move away.

"H-how do I do that?" Joy asked as her precarious situation sank in. She was afraid to move, to even breathe, fearing she'd instantly fall through the ice.

"Go down on your hands and knees, then stretch out so you're lying flat on the ice." Quinn's voice was calm. "I know your wrists are bound together, so you'll need to try and place your palms on the ice as flat as possible."

Tarin shot an incredulous look at his brother. "What? Are you sure about this?"

"I'm with the Coast Guard," Quinn said. "I know what I'm talking about."

Tarin turned to smile reassuringly at her as if she wasn't near death for the second time in ten minutes. "Do as he says, Joy."

Joy lowered herself down until she was on her hands and knees. More cracking sounds sent a shaft of fear to her heart. Icy cold water came up through the snow, pooling beneath her hands and knees. "I'm breaking through!"

"I know, but that's why you need to stretch out on your stomach," Quinn said. "I know it's scary, but that's the best way to distribute your weight over the ice. Do you understand what I'm saying? Your hands and knees are holding all your weight and that provides a stress point that will cause you to break through the ice."

"The ice is already broken, water is coming up through the cracks," she protested as she followed his commands. Seconds later, she was lying on her stomach. The icy water mingled with the layer of snow covering the ice. "It's cold," she said, her teeth chattering.

"It's okay, it won't be for long. I'm coming to get you." Quinn lowered himself down onto the ground so that he was also on his stomach.

"Wait!" Tarin stripped off his jacket. "You might need to use this as a rope to pull her closer to you. I don't think the ice will hold both of you, even with your weight distributed over a larger area."

"Good idea." Quinn took the jacket in one hand as he shimmied across the ice toward Joy. More cracking noises made Tarin's brother stop.

Joy knew the ice was about to break into dozens of pieces. She tried to slide herself forward, but the cold water was soaking through her jacket, sapping her strength.

"Grab hold." Quinn tossed the jacket toward her while hanging on to one of the long sleeves. It landed about three inches from her bound wrists. "Come on, Joy, you can do it."

She gathered her strength and scooted forward, grabbing the end of the sleeve with her cold fingers. "G-got it."

"Hold tight and try to relax," Quinn called as he slowly

and carefully tugged Joy across the ice toward him, one slow inch at a time, pausing every so often to wiggle backward to get closer to the shore.

She fixed her gaze on Tarin, who looked scared to death. She wanted to reassure him this would work, to tell him how much she loved him, but her teeth were chattering so hard she couldn't speak.

There was another loud crack.

Her hips and legs fell completely through the ice into the water.

"Joy!" Tarin's hoarse shout sounded like he was far away, and she wondered if she'd soon fall the rest of the way through the ice. For a strange moment, she thought about Jack being in the water during the movie, *Titanic*. Her legs were numb; she couldn't feel anything but cold.

So cold.

"Get her out of there, Quinn!"

"I'm trying!" Quinn's expression was grim.

She wasn't sure how much longer she could hold on. Tarin bent down and grabbed his brother's ankles and pulled. She felt herself moving forward, but because of the numbness, she couldn't tell if she was coming out of the water or not.

Yet she soon realized she was moving closer to shore. Glancing behind her, she saw that her legs were out of the water now, and she was sliding across the ice. Tarin relentlessly pulled on his brother's ankles as if he were a work horse, his face growing red with the effort.

"You're doing great, Tarin," Quinn said. "Another foot and we'll be off the ice!"

Tarin didn't respond, his efforts focused on getting them to shore.

"You did it! We're off the ice!" Quinn's hoarse shout had Tarin dropping his ankles and rushing toward her.

"Joy? Can you stand? We need to get you warm, okay?"

"Y-yes." She understood what he was saying, but her limbs weren't cooperating. Tarin pulled out a knife, cut through the binds around her wrists, then bent to lift her upright.

"I'll help," Quinn said, rising to his feet.

"Grab her feet," Tarin said. "We need to get her into the car!"

Her teeth continued to chatter, her legs still feeling numb. As Tarin and Quinn carried her past the marina building, she caught a glimpse of Kevin lying on the ground surrounded by blood.

"I-is h-he, d-ea-ead?" It was strangely difficult to speak. As if she couldn't get her lips to follow her commands.

"Yes." Tarin waited for Quinn to wrench open the back seat of the vehicle. "Get her inside, we'll need a blanket too."

Quinn awkwardly climbed into the back seat while holding on to her feet. A minute later, she was sitting on the back seat with Tarin crowded next to her. It took her a minute to realize he was unbuttoning her jeans.

"W-what a-are yo-u do-ing?" She batted at his hands with the strength of a mosquito.

"These wet things must come off, you're losing body heat. Don't worry, we'll cover you with the blanket."

The grim intensity of Tarin's gaze made it clear he was still concerned about her welfare. She knew it was foolish to worry about her modesty at a time like this. She tried to lift her butt up to help him get the wet jeans off, but her attempt was feeble at best. Once he had wrenched her jeans off, along with her shoes and socks, he worked on her wet jacket too. Finally, he wrapped her in a red and black flannel blanket.

Quinn was behind the wheel, cranking the heat. When Tarin had her wrapped in the blanket, he pulled her into his arms and held her tight.

"I almost lost you," he whispered against her hair.

"I-I kn-ow." Her teeth were still chattering, but the warmth radiating from Tarin's body was a blessing. A prickly sensation in her legs indicated they were warming up too. She rested her head on his chest, soaking up the warmth with an appreciation she'd never known before. "I'm s-sorry."

"Don't apologize, it's my fault." She hated to hear the guilt in his tone.

"Y-you didn't kn-know Kevin was i-involved."

"No, that was a shock, but I shouldn't have left you alone. Not for one second."

"Give yourself a break, Tarin," Quinn said from the front seat. "The motel should have been safe. If I hadn't brought clothes, he probably wouldn't have found her. If anyone is at fault, it's me."

"I told you to bring them," Tarin said.

"Stop beating yourself up. It's over and done," Quinn repeated. The wail of sirens interrupted the conversation between the two brothers. "Looks like Brady sent the cavalry, they should be here soon."

Joy knew that this moment alone with Tarin wouldn't last long. She lifted her head to gaze up at him. "Thank you for rescuing me."

"I'm grateful we made it in time." A tiny frown puckered his brow. "Why were you running toward the lake?"

She flushed. "Stupid move on my part, wasn't it? When I heard the chopper, I took off, thinking maybe Kevin wouldn't expect me to run toward the water. With the snow covering the ice, I didn't realize how far out I'd gone until you called out to me." She grimaced, then somberly admitted. "Deep down, I thought that if I was going to die today, the icy water might be a better alternative to being shot with bullets."

"I've never been so scared in my life when your legs fell through the ice." His fingertips lightly brushed across her cheek. "God was watching over you today."

She nodded, then blurted, "I love you, Tarin."

His brown eyes widened. "Joy, you've just been through a harrowing experience, and . . ."

"I love you. You don't have to love me back, I know your heart belongs to Caroline." She ignored the muffled cough from Quinn in the front seat who was obviously listening in. "I just wanted you to know. I love you. And I'm so glad God brought you into my life."

Before Tarin could say anything more, three squads shot across the parking lot toward them.

"They'll want to talk to you, bro," Quinn said as he slid out from behind the wheel.

"Yeah." Tarin eased away, taking a moment to tuck the plaid blanket securely around her. "Stay here where it's warm."

She nodded, watching as Tarin and Quinn crossed over to join the officers. She didn't regret telling him her feelings. Maybe someday Tarin would set aside his grief and open his heart to love. If not with her, then with someone else.

He deserved that, and more.

JOY LOVED HIM. Tarin knew she might not have meant the words, but they brought a glow of happiness just the same. Still, he focused on the officers who were looking for answers regarding the shooting death of Kevin Creek.

"I shot at him to protect Joy Munson," Tarin said. "He had a gun, and I could tell he was going to use it."

"I shot him," Quinn argued. "I saw him with his gun aimed at Joy too."

The officers looked from Tarin to Quinn, then back at Tarin. "Okay, so you both shot him. Maybe you should start at the very beginning? Why would Kevin Creek want to kill Joy Munson?"

Tarin swallowed a frustrated sigh. Telling the entire story would take too long, and he'd only have to rehash it all over again when the detectives arrived on the scene. "My brother Brady Finnegan is an FBI agent, and he's been involved with this case from a federal level. I need to talk to him first."

That only made the officer scowl. "Yeah, well, this dead guy is in our jurisdiction, so unless you want me to haul you both to the precinct, you'll tell me what is going on!"

He wanted nothing more than to hand the entire thing over to Quinn so he could go back to the car to talk with Joy. Sighing heavily and shivering in the cold without his jacket, he was about to gesture to the SUV when a sedan pulled up. Tarin could tell they were the detectives and was glad he'd only have to tell the story once.

"I'm Detective Miles Callahan, and this is my partner, Detective Erwin," the sandy-haired guy resembled Marc Callahan.

"Detective Tarin Finnegan, and my brother Quinn." Tarin shook both detectives' hands. "Is Marc Callahan your brother?"

"Yeah, why?" Miles asked.

"He's working this case with my brother Brady, who is also a fed." He shivered again. "Listen, my coat is soaked with water, can we sit inside the SUV to talk?"

"Sure, but it sounds like I should get in touch with the feds too." Miles appeared interested in the connection. "Ironic that your brother is working with mine, huh?"

"I suppose you're aware of the DNA connection too," Tarin said as he scooted into the back seat with Joy. Quinn stayed outside to talk with Erwin while Callahan sat in the front seat, turning to face him.

"Yep. Crazy about the similar professions," Miles said with a wry grin. "Two federal agents, two detectives, what are the chances of that?"

"Don't forget we have cops and firefighters in common too," Tarin said. "The Finnegans have you outnumbered, though. Nine of us to your six."

Miles shook his head. "And I thought having five siblings was bad, but eight? Wow."

"Tell me about it." He inched closer to Joy. "Joy, this is Detective Miles Callahan. He's related to Marc, and we need to fill him in on what happened five years ago and how that led up to the events today."

"Okay." She managed a smile. "It's a long story, though."

"I have plenty of time," Miles said reassuringly.

Tarin explained about how he and Dave had been called to the scene of Ken Munson's death, which they now believed to have been staged to look like a suicide. After describing the events that happened over the past two days, he finished with the shooting of Sue Melius in the Baker's Best Café and the subsequent arrest of Craig Washington, the pharmacist.

"I was lulled into a sense of safety and stupidly left Joy alone in the motel room to meet up with Quinn. When I returned, she was gone."

"Not your fault, Tarin," Miles quickly interjected.

It was, but he let it go for now. "Joy can tell you what happened from there."

Joy did so, explaining how Kevin Creek bragged about his IT skills, how he'd bugged her phone and her computer long ago, and had therefore known about her meeting with Tarin about her brother's case.

Tarin tried not to feel guilty for suspecting his partner, Dave, or DEA Agent Doug Bridges of being dirty. He'd really believed only a cop with connections could have pulled this off.

Not an IT guy who was in on the drug scheme.

"Wait a minute, I wonder if Creek somehow used his connections at the hospital to help create the fake prescriptions."

"That's a good point, I guess the feds may have to look into that possibility," Miles said thoughtfully. "But it stands to reason he's involved from an IT perspective, given the skills he has."

"I should have considered he might be part of it." Tarin wondered how many other clues he'd missed. If anything had happened to Joy, he'd never have been able to forgive himself.

"How could you know that?" Joy asked. "I didn't even know what kind of computer hacking skills he had."

"How did he find you at the motel?" Miles asked.

"I heard a buzzing noise outside the café," Joy said. "I didn't see anything, though."

"A drone!" Tarin wanted to smack himself in the head. "I should have thought of that! He's a computer guy, he no doubt used the drone to tail us long enough to realize where we were going." Tarin hated to realize just how badly he'd underestimated their foe.

"I should have mentioned the sound," Joy said, her expression dark with guilt. "He also got a key to the room, probably from the maid. While he was driving me here to the marina, he was careful not to say too much. Other than explaining I needed to be silenced, he didn't verbally admit to killing Sue Melius or taking those other shots at me."

"His weapon will tell the tale," Tarin said. "I'm sure the ammo in his gun will match the shell casings found at two of the scenes. And now that we know about the drone, we can look for that too."

"Why did he bring you here to the marina?" Miles asked.

"I don't know. I told him the lake was iced over, but I think he had some sort of plan to shoot me and push me beneath the ice so my body wouldn't be found until spring." She shivered, and Tarin slipped his arm around her shoulders. "I think his idea may have worked as I was out on the ice and nearly fell through."

"Really?" Miles's eyebrows arched. "I'm glad you were able to get out."

"Tarin and his brother Quinn pulled me across the ice. Without them, I wouldn't be here."

The near miss still bothered him. So close. He'd come so close to losing Joy forever.

"Kevin was different from the man I remember. He was so cold and calculating, it was frightening. I can't believe I dated him."

Tarin shared a look with Miles and knew they were both thinking the same thing. Kevin may have purposefully gone after Joy, probably to find out about her brother and his commitment, or lack thereof, to the drug scheme. And after his death and her insisting he hadn't killed himself, he had ditched her.

"Hey, it's over. You're safe now." Tarin hugged her.

"I'm sorry you had to go through all of that," Miles agreed.

After another brief discussion, Miles left them in the SUV to talk to his partner. The detective side of him wanted to follow Miles to see what other evidence they might find, but it wasn't his case.

And he was happy to stay right where he was.

"I—uh need to go home. See how much damage there is to my condo, then call my insurance company. Oh, and pick up my car from the shop." Joy sounded exhausted but determined.

Every cell in his body rejected that idea. "You can do all of that tomorrow. I think it's better if you come back to the Finnegan homestead for a few days." *Or longer*, he silently added. "You deserve time to relax after this."

"I don't want to be a bother," she protested.

"Please, Joy." He gently tipped her chin with his index finger so she was facing him. "Please come home with me."

Her hazel eyes clung to his. "You don't live there."

"I'll use Aiden's room, and once he returns, I can sleep on the sofa." He wanted desperately to believe she really loved him, but as a cop, he knew that she might just have a sense of hero worship. Or maybe she wouldn't want to be with a cop at all. She had mentioned not liking the way they were in harm's way. "The danger is over. I'm sure once Craig Washington learns of Kevin's death, he'll realize the gig is up. Especially if Creek was the one supplying the doctor's names, DEA numbers, and other prescription information. Without him, the entire operation falls apart."

"I know the danger is finally over, and that is a huge relief." She sighed, then looked away. "But there's a lot that needs to get done so that I'm able to move on with my life."

"A few days is all I'm asking." Tarin didn't want her to leave.

"You've been great through all this, but I don't want to burden you and your family any more than I already have."

"I love you." He hadn't intended to tell her, but he couldn't help it. "I loved Caroline, but she's gone. I didn't expect to care about anyone else the same way, but the truth is, I've fallen for you, Joy."

She turned back to face him. "You don't have to say that just because I did. I could never live up to Caroline. She was a cop, like you, but I'm a boring accountant. This"—she waved a hand toward the sea of squads and cops—"isn't normal. After the excitement dies down, you'll be bored with me."

"No way, that's not true. I love you," he repeated firmly. "I'm the one who is concerned about your feelings, Joy. You've been in danger nonstop, and I'm the one who's been at your side. The truth is, it's not easy dating a cop. Oh, plenty of women think it's cool until they're faced with long hours and cases that I can't talk about, not to mention the danger." He needed to be completely honest with her. "I'm worried that once you see the real me, you won't be very interested in spending time with me long-term either."

"I know you better than any other man I've ever dated." She smiled. "I know you're honorable, kind, stubborn, and determined to do the right thing no matter what. And I love your family, too, at least the siblings I've met."

"Don't forget the cousins you've met," he teased. "Elly is going to be so jealous that you met Marc and Miles Callahan before she did."

That made her laugh softly. "I love you, Tarin. And I'd love to give a relationship with you a try as long as you promise to let me know if you grow bored with me." A shadow darkened her eyes, and he knew that was Kevin talking.

"Don't compare me to the man who tried to kill you." He winced when he realized that came out stronger than he'd intended. "I'm sorry, Joy, but he's clearly a bad guy. I love you. I care about you. I will never hurt you, and I also promise to be honest with you."

"Okay, then I would also ask that you don't compare me to Caroline either, although I know she was perfect for you."

"She wasn't," he protested. "Caroline and I bonded over the job, and we let that closeness turn into something more. But she's gone, and while I cared for her and will miss her, I promise you I'm not obsessed with her memory."

She nodded. "Okay, thanks for that. I love you, Tarin. I will never hurt you, and I promise to be honest, no matter what." She paused, then added, "And I'll stay with you at the Finnegan homestead for a few days as long as Rhy, Elly, and the others don't mind."

"They won't." He smiled broadly, then brought her close for another kiss.

She melted against him as he deepened the kiss, showering her with all the love welling up inside of him.

The cold blast of air from someone opening the car door interrupted them. Tarin reluctantly lifted his head and scowled. "What?"

"Sorry to bother you," Quinn said with a cheeky grin that belied his words. "But Marc and Brady are here, they'd like to talk to you both."

It wasn't fair for him to be annoyed with them, but he

wanted to get Joy to his family's home. "Okay, fine. But we're staying in here. They can come to us."

Quinn's grin widened, but he backed up and said, "They're all yours."

Brady and Marc Callahan took the two front seats. It wasn't the best setup to do an interview, but they didn't protest. Tarin quickly reiterated what had transpired, with Joy adding her part. Brady looked upset upon hearing how close Quinn and Joy had come to falling through the ice.

"Thanks for filling in the details, especially about Kevin Creek's tech skills," Brady said. "They found his drone in the back of the black sedan, so that's good. The maid at the motel was knocked unconscious, but she'll survive. We also verified that Doug Bridges is clean; he really was working with Sue Melius on the case. Kevin Creek was one of the missing pieces of the puzzle. Now we'll have to get a warrant for the hospital's IT records related to whatever databases Creek hacked into."

"Yeah, that won't be fun," Callahan muttered.

"No, they'll kick and scream about patient confidentiality, but we'll get what we need. I'm sure they don't want their good name dragged through the mud."

"Did Washington give you anything else?" Tarin asked.

"He admitted to getting information from Creek, and he knew there were other pharmacies involved too. He gave us the doctors' names, which we had from the spreadsheet Sue Melius had tucked in her safe." Brady glanced at Marc. "Now that we know Creek is dead, we can probably squeeze more information out of him."

"Now that will be fun," Callahan agreed. Then he turned toward Joy. "I know you've been through a lot today, but I want to thank you for pushing forward on your brother's case. As awful as all of this was for you, the end result is that we'll be able to take thousands of narcotics off the street."

"I—you're welcome." Joy sighed. "I know my brother will be happy to know that Craig and the others will be held accountable for their crimes."

"They will." Brady shot Tarin a knowing look. "That's all we have for now, but I hope I get to see you again very soon. Like maybe at family dinner?"

"Oh, I don't know . . ." Joy looked a little panicked.

"You'll love family dinner," Tarin said, giving her another hug. "And the family will love you as much as I do."

"Wow, the two oldest Finnegans are in love, who would have thought?" Brady teased.

"Oh, leave them alone," Marc said, slapping a hand on Brady's shoulder. "From what I hear, they deserve to be happy."

"They do," Brady agreed, his expression turning somber. "Take her home, Tarin."

"I plan to."

After Brady and Marc left, he turned toward Joy. "Don't be intimidated by the family, they like to joke around, but they don't mean any harm."

"I love your family," Joy said firmly. "You wouldn't be the man you are without them."

He nodded slowly. "That is very true." He kissed her again, reveling in the bright light of happiness Joy brought upon them.

Secretly vowing to never let her go.

EPILOGUE

Two weeks later...

Joy's condo repairs were scheduled to be finished by the weekend, and as she stood in her room in the Finnegan homestead, she knew she would miss the place.

Not that living among Finnegans coming and going at all hours of the day and night was easy. But soon she welcomed the somewhat controlled chaos that Rhy, Elly, Alanna, and Aiden brought.

Tarin had been wonderful, and even though their lives had fallen into a routine as they'd returned to work, he hadn't seemed bored with her yet.

Tonight, he told her they needed to run an errand, and he'd be there to pick her up right after work. Intrigued, she dressed casually, then headed downstairs to the kitchen, which she learned was the heart of the Finnegan homestead.

"You look nice," Elly said with a smile.

"Thanks." She adored the youngest Finnegan sibling.

"Will you and Tarin be here for dinner?"

"Um, I'm not sure. He mentioned running an errand,

but I'm not sure how long that will take. We'll have to ask when he gets here."

"Oh, sure." Elly gestured to the kitchen window. "That's probably him now."

A few minutes later, Tarin entered the room. "Hey, ready to go?"

"Yes." She pulled on her coat. "Elly was wondering about dinner."

Tarin glanced at his watch. "We should be back by six. Count us in, Elly."

"Okay." Elly almost looked disappointed by the news.

Once they were settled in the SUV, she asked, "Where are we going?"

"It's a surprise." He flashed her a grin.

"Okay." This was unusual, normally he wasn't secretive about stuff. She was even more confused when he pulled into the parking lot of a jewelry store. "Are you picking up something for your sisters?"

"I am interested in your opinion." He slid out from behind the wheel and came around to open her door.

Christmas was a long way away, so she was trying to figure out which of the sisters, Kyleigh, Alanna, or Elly, had a birthday coming up. No one had mentioned a birthday, but then again, there were nine kids to keep track of. Although now that she thought about it, Aiden and Alanna were twins, so there were only eight birthdays.

"Ah, Mr. Finnegan, it's good to see you again." The older man in a suit beamed. "And this must be—"

"Joy Munson, and Joy, this is Randolph Powers, the owner of the store."

"It's nice to meet you," she said.

Tarin cleared his throat as Randolph pulled out a small

velvet case from behind the counter. Tarin opened the box and turned toward her.

Then he dropped to one knee. "Joy, I love you. You've brought me so much happiness over these past few weeks. I'm not sure what type of ring you like since I couldn't find any jewelry at your condo, so if you don't like this, we'll pick out something else." He held up a simple diamond solitaire ring. "Will you please marry me?"

"Yes, Tarin!" She laughed, tears of joy welling in her eyes. "A thousand times, yes! I love you, and the ring is perfect. I'll be honored to be your wife."

"Ah, it's settled, then," Randolph said, beaming with pride.

Tarin rose, took the ring out of the case, and slid it onto the third finger of her left hand. "I love you so much," he murmured.

"I love you too." She wound her arms around his neck and kissed him.

After a long moment, Randolph cleared his throat. "Would you like a gift bag?"

Joy burst out laughing. Tarin did too. "No thank you," she managed. "I think I'll wear this home."

Tarin's gaze was tender. "Speaking of home, I think we should find a new place to live, one that suits both of us. Maybe something close to the Finnegan homestead. Once your condo is finished, we can put it on the market, and I'll put my house up for sale too." Then he grinned. "But that's an errand for another day. I love you, Joy."

"I'd like that, and I love you too." A new home for the two of them sounded perfect. "I hope we still get to do family dinner, though."

He chuckled. "We will." He kissed her again, and she

couldn't imagine anything better than becoming a Finnegan.

What a blessing that God had brought her and Tarin together.

I HOPE you enjoyed Tarin and Joy's story in *Seeking Justice*. I'm having a blast with the Finnegans and their cousins the Callahans. Are you ready for Kyleigh and Baxter's story in *Protection Detail*? Click Here!

DEAR READER

I'm having so much fun with my new series! Finnegan's First Responders is about nine siblings who all serve the public, putting their lives on the line to save others. They also soon realize they are related to the Callahan family! For those of you who enjoyed my Callahan Confidential series, you'll love catching up with members of the family as they cross paths and support the Finnegans. And you know there will be a large family reunion at the end.

If you enjoyed Tarin and Joy's story in *Seeking Justice*, take a moment to check out *Protection Detail*, Kyleigh and Baxter's story. I'm already loving the Finnegans, and I hope you are too. Anyone choosing to purchase any e-books or audiobooks (including these new Finnegan books) directly from my website will receive a 15% discount by using the code **LauraScott15** at checkout.

I adore hearing from my readers! I can be found through my website at https://www.laurascottbooks.com, via Facebook at https://www.facebook.com/LauraScott Books, Instagram at https://www.instagram.com/laurascott books/, and Twitter https://twitter.com/laurascottbooks.

Also, take a moment to sign up for my monthly newsletter to learn about my new book releases! All subscribers receive a free novella not available for purchase on any platform.

Until next time,

Laura Scott

PS. Keep reading for a preview of *Protection Detail*.

PROTECTION DETAIL

Chapter One

Assistant District Attorney Baxter Scala strode purposefully along the sidewalk leading to the Milwaukee County Courthouse. He despised being late, and while his attorney ID would allow him to skip ahead of the line of people waiting to pass through the metal detector, he would still have to elbow his way through the crowds. Unfortunately, prosecuting T-Turbo, a famous musician, for murder had drawn local and national media attention.

A cold March wind buffeted his back, pushing him along the sidewalk. As he approached the steps of the courthouse, he saw a skinny homeless guy sitting along the sidewalk. Bundled against the wind, his knit cap pulled low on his head, the guy didn't glance up at him but held out an empty cup. Bax saw him there on a regular basis, no matter how cold or snowy the winter weather.

He pulled a five-dollar bill from his pocket and stuffed it into the cup, then kept going. The guy didn't acknowledge his donation the way he usually did. Not that it mattered. Bax was due in court soon. The minute he approached the main doorway of the courthouse, several reporters recognized him. They rushed forward, sticking their microphones in his face. It was all he could do not to smack them away.

"ADA Scala, do you have any thoughts about the murder case against T-Turbo as you prepare for the pretrial hearing today?"

Yeah, where do you come up with these ridiculous questions? He worked hard to keep his expression neutral. "No comment."

"ADA Scala, are you concerned about T-Turbo's claim that he has an alibi for the time frame of the murder?"

Oh, you mean his new groupie girlfriend who would lie through her teeth for him, despite the fact that he murdered his former girlfriend? "No comment." Bax resolutely pushed through the crowd, avoiding eye contact as he headed inside the tan brick building.

Holding up his ID, he made his way along the left side of the corridor, passing the dozens of people waiting in line. Some were jurors, others were witnesses, others were there because they had a civil or criminal hearing of their own. The pool of jury members he'd pick from during the process of voir dire wouldn't report in until the following morning, so he didn't have to worry about stumbling across a potential juror.

The two Milwaukee County Sheriff Deputies manning the metal detector nodded at him. One stepped forward to wave a handheld detection device over him before stepping back and allowing him to pass.

He found it interesting they never looked for a weapon inside his briefcase. Granted, if he was ever caught with one, he'd lose his job. Still, he couldn't help thinking that if someone was determined to wreak havoc inside the hallowed walls, it wouldn't be as difficult to get a weapon inside the courtroom via an attorney.

Avoiding the crowded elevators, he headed for the stairs. The criminal courtrooms were located on the fourth floor of the five-story building. He didn't mind the exercise, and he didn't like the idea of being stuck in an elevator with a cuffed criminal or worse, potential jurors. Even a casual conversation with a juror could cause a mistrial.

His case against T-Turbo was scheduled for the next two weeks and would be heard before the Honorable Judge Glenn Dugan. One of the better judges in his opinion, despite their clashes in the past. They didn't always see eye to eye on legal issues, but Dugan was a stickler for rules. Bax liked that about him. The rules tended to help the prosecutors more so than the defense.

He entered the courtroom and nodded at Deputy Kyleigh Finnegan standing near the doorway. "Good morning."

"Good morning," she replied.

Not smart to allow a pretty face to be a distraction, especially in the most notorious case to cross his desk in the past three years. Yet he couldn't help but notice Kyleigh's pale skin, large brown eyes, and curly red hair that she pulled back from her face in a no-nonsense bun. He knew from previous experience, having seen her over the past two months, that by the end of the day, several of those red curls would escape the band and frame her beautiful face.

Not for the first time, he'd wondered what had drawn her to a career in law enforcement. Did she like being stuck in courtrooms all day? It seemed to him to be a relatively boring job. Then again, maybe she liked the break from being out on the streets.

What aspects of her career Kyleigh did and didn't enjoy were none of his business. As soon as T-Turbo's lawyers showed up—*all three of them*, he thought—Deputy Finnegan would take up a position near the judge's chambers.

He set his briefcase on the glossy wooden desk and glanced at his watch, wondering where Jack Jones, his junior ADA was. He'd given the younger attorney strict rules about not talking to the reporters, so that better not be what was holding him up.

"Excuse me, ADA Scala?" Deputy Finnegan's husky voice startled him. He spun around to find her standing close by.

"Yes?" He frowned when he saw the envelope in her hand. He could clearly see his name typed on the front of the envelope, which he thought was odd. "What is that?"

"I just noticed this on the floor inside the doorway." She frowned as she handed him the envelope. "Did you drop it?"

"No." He stared at it for a moment, a shiver of apprehension sliding down his spine. He quickly opened the envelope, peering cautiously inside to make sure there was nothing more than paper in there. He'd heard about anthrax letters going through the mail shortly after 9/11, targeting state senators and other elected officials. No worries here, though. He pulled out the single sheet of paper that contained one short sentence typed from a computer.

If you know what's good for you, you'll drop the murder charge.

"Is something wrong?" Deputy Finnegan asked. A hint of lavender wafted toward him.

Scowling, he held up the note. "Are you sure you didn't see who left this?"

"I'm sure." She frowned and lifted her hand to the radio clipped to her collar. "Howell? This is Finnegan. I need someone to look at the video cameras for the footage outside Judge Dugan's courtroom to ID a perp who slipped a threatening note under the door."

"Roger that" was the response.

"I don't like it. This must be related to the T-Turbo trial." She spoke in a low voice. "I know the media has been all over the news, but leaving a threatening note? That's a little over the top."

He shoved the note and envelope toward her. The tone was threatening, but he wasn't worried. The camera would pick up whoever had done this. "It's probably just a fanatic looking for his or her thirty seconds of fame."

Deputy Finnegan grimaced as she took the evidence. "I'll let Judge Dugan know. He may request extra protection, especially once the trial starts."

"That's fine, but again, I'm not concerned about a note." He found himself mesmerized by her warm brown eyes and forced himself to look away. "You'll let me know what the video outside the courtroom shows?"

"Of course." She carefully slid the note and envelope into a plastic bag. "We'll check for prints too."

"Great, thanks." He drummed up a smile. "I just hope this isn't an indication of how the rest of the day will progress."

"I hear you," she agreed.

The courtroom door opened, and they both jumped around to face the newcomer. Bax relaxed when he saw Jack Jones. "It's about time."

"Sorry, those reporters wouldn't let me through." Jack

was young, twenty-six to Bax's thirty-four, but on days like today, Bax felt decades older.

"I told you, don't stop or ask politely, just bulldoze your way through." He tried not to let his exasperation show. He didn't mind having a young protégé sitting in as second chair, but it would help if Jack heeded his advice. The kid was book smart and could perform legal case searches like a pro. But common sense? Not so much. "Sit down, we need to talk."

He decided against telling Jack about the letter. For one thing, it had been addressed to him. Everyone knew he was the lead prosecutor on the case. But the biggest issue was that he was afraid Jack would overreact to the threat. The kid needed more real-world experience, which was why he was there.

This wasn't Bax's first weird letter, but he could admit that they'd never shown up at the courthouse before.

Whatever. He needed to stay focused on the case. Convicting T-Turbo of murder was all that mattered.

The rest of the morning passed quickly as he and T-Turbo's team of high-priced lawyers worked through the long list of pretrial motions. Judge Dugan granted some of Bax's motions but dismissed others. Dugan did the same with Ward Gorski the lead defense attorney's motions. It was no surprise that Judge Dugan often split the baby down the middle, essentially making both sides unhappy. Another sign of a good and impartial judge, in his humble opinion.

If the judge was worried about the anonymous note, he didn't mention it. Which was fine with Bax. That was the least of his worries.

He'd won his motion to include the victim's statements prior to her death, but he'd lost on another equally important motion. In his mind, he was already switching around his prosecution strategy.

He kept Jack at the table, speaking in low tones about the next round of case law Jack needed to find, until the trio of defense lawyers had vacated the room. When the area was clear, he stood and packed his briefcase. He was about to follow Jack out when Deputy Finnegan flagged him down.

"Excuse me, ADA Scala?" A wisp of red hair had come out of her bun and framed her face. As always, the stray curls made him wish he could see Kyleigh with her hair down.

"Bax? Need me to stay?" Jack asked.

"No, go ahead. I'll meet up with you later." He turned toward Finnegan. "Do you have news about the letter?"

"Only bad news, I'm afraid." She sighed. "The envelope was pushed under the door by a Caucasian man with a closely trimmed beard. He wore a ball cap pulled low on his head and baggy clothes. He never once looked up at the cameras, almost as if he knew where they were located. They're going to try to run him through our facial recognition program, but I wouldn't hold your breath. I don't think there's enough there to capture a reasonable likeness."

"Any age estimate on the guy?"

"Anywhere from eighteen to thirty." She pulled out her phone and stepped closer so he could see the image on the screen. "Does he look familiar?"

Bax peered at the person who'd been caught on camera. He bore a resemblance the homeless guy outside the courthouse, except that man's beard had reached all the way down to his chest, while the letter perp had a trimmed beard. Still, the clothes were exactly as he remembered. "There was a homeless guy outside when I came in; I dropped a five-dollar bill in his cup. If he'd trimmed his beard, this could be him."

Her brown eyes widened. "Show me."

He glanced at his watch again and tried not to sigh. "Okay. I need to grab something to eat. I have a meeting with a witness right after lunch."

"I understand, this shouldn't take long." She fell into step beside him, using her radio once more to alert the other deputies that she was leaving her post for lunch.

"I hope you don't mind stairs." He gestured toward them.

"Not at all." Her quick answer made him think she shared his aversion to closed-in elevator spaces.

The stairwells were notoriously empty, which was nice. When they hit the ground level, though, they had to slow down to navigate through the crowds. The courthouse had a café that was always jammed at the noon hour, which was why he avoided it.

Outside, he was thankful to realize the slew of reporters had thinned. Or maybe they were out there but put off because of Deputy Finnegan's presence beside him.

"This way," he said, heading down toward the sidewalk. Then he abruptly stopped and looked around.

The homeless guy was gone.

*

"He was right here." ADA Scala scowled and waved a hand. "I see him all the time. I usually give him a five or whatever I have on me."

"I believe you." Kyleigh didn't doubt the lawyer's memory. Bax was smart and savvy. She'd watched him go after criminals in the past, and nothing seemed to get past him. To be honest, she secretly admired his dogged determination to put criminals behind bars. "Seems likely he's our letter perp."

"But he's here just about every day," Bax insisted. "Why would he suddenly write a threatening letter?"

She arched a brow. "He didn't write it, how could he? The only access he'd have to a computer would be at the library. Which isn't far, but I'm sure someone paid him to go inside the building and to slide the note under the courtroom door."

He did not look happy with that thought but nodded. "You're right. He'd have done the deed for cash, no questions asked."

"Exactly." Kyleigh glanced around the busy pedestrian area around the courthouse. There were lots of people milling about. There was absolutely no way she'd be able to find the person responsible. "You should watch your back, counselor. The case has drawn a lot of media attention, most of it not sympathetic to your office."

"No lie," he muttered. "Thanks for your concern, but I'll be fine."

When he turned away, she made a snap decision to follow. Which earned her another annoyed piercing look from his intense blue eyes. She stared right back. "I don't mind escorting you to the administrative building."

"There's no need for that," he protested. "Letter writers rarely go as far as committing assault and battery."

Logically, she agreed with him, but the note had bothered her. Maybe because of the way the perp had used the homeless guy to deliver it. Judge Dugan hadn't liked it either, but he also hadn't asked for additional protection for himself or the ADA.

Yet.

"I understand, but it's my job to take any threat to you or the judge very seriously." She kept pace alongside him.

"The threat was aimed at me, not the judge."

"Same difference." This wasn't the time to split hairs. "You mentioned stopping for lunch?"

"I was going to grab something at the café outside the admin building." He sounded cranky.

"Really? That's where I was planning to grab lunch, too, it's a great place." She grinned. "How convenient that we have similar taste in food."

He shot her a death glare but didn't say anything more. Kyleigh figured having a deputy with him might be ruining his image. She didn't know much about Baxter Scala on a personal level, other than overhearing a terse phone call several weeks ago with his ex-fiancée. What was her name? Tara? No, Tamera.

On some level, she felt sorry for the woman. A guy as handsome as ADA Scala could have whoever he wanted. It must have been heartbreaking to have him break off their engagement, although in the conversation she'd heard, he'd told her to keep the ring.

From the wry expression on his face, she assumed Tamera intended to do so anyway, no matter what Baxter said.

That made her think of her oldest brother Rhy's upcoming wedding to Devon. And her second oldest brother Tarin's recent engagement to Joy. She had a total of eight siblings, most of them younger. Rhy and Tarin were the oldest, and ten years ago, they'd both moved back home after their parents died. She'd pitched in to help, too, as did the others. Elly, the youngest, had been only fourteen at the time, and the twins, Aiden and Alanna, had been seventeen. The eldest Finnegans had willingly put their personal lives on hold to keep the family together.

Until recently. Over the past two months, her two oldest brothers had fallen like a ton of bricks for the women they were determined to protect.

Personally, she was thrilled for them. They deserved to be happy, and both Devon and Joy were great additions to the Finnegan family.

Kyleigh might be next in line age wise, but she didn't harbor any illusions of finding love the way Rhy and Tarin had. The single guys she worked with were more interested in quick hookups, not long-term commitments. And her former non cop boyfriend Rick Atkins had basically given her an ultimatum. Rick had demanded she choose between him and her job.

Not a tough decision to choose her career. Rick was an idiot; there was no way she was going to walk away. Being a deputy was more than a job. It was a call to service, a trait that had been ingrained in her and her siblings by their parents. Every Finnegan was involved in serving the public in some way. Well, except for Elly who was still training to become an EMT.

"So, tell me what's good here?" she asked as they stood in line.

"I thought you were a regular?" Scala scowled.

She shrugged. "Have to say it's been a while."

He sighed and waved a hand at the menu overhead. "Everything is good. The only thing I haven't tried is the veggie burger."

She wrinkled her nose. "Not a fan of fake meat."

He chuckled. The sound surprised her. Obviously, she'd only watched him in the courtroom, and the cases he prosecuted were generally not funny. "Me either," he said, then stepped forward when it was his turn.

ADA Scala ordered a BLT sandwich to go and a bottle of water. After paying, he stepped to the side, moving down a couple of feet while looking down at his phone. Working? She had to assume the T-Turbo case was his main priority for the next two weeks.

Hers, too, now that there had been a threat received in the courtroom.

Her stint at the courthouse would last through the end of June, then she'd be rotated over to patrolling and guarding the airport. Switching assignments helped to keep boredom at bay, but she liked being in court, watching as the DA's office worked with the police to hold the bad guys accountable for their crimes.

Not that justice was always served. Sometimes the bad guys walked, which was difficult to comprehend. She knew that taking a case to the jury meant there was always a chance of an acquittal. Still, it was still a sucker punch to the gut to watch. She found herself hoping and praying that wouldn't happen with the T-Turbo case.

Her stomach rumbled with hunger, and while the BLT sounded good, she decided to get a turkey club to go along with a bottle of water. She pulled out her credit card to pay, but the woman behind the register waved her off.

"The gentleman paid for your meal."

"Oh, uh, thanks." Kyleigh could feel her face burning with embarrassment, the curse of having red hair and fair skin. She glanced at Scala who'd tucked his phone away. "I didn't follow you here so you could pay my way."

"I know." He shrugged as if his kind gesture was no big deal. She remembered what he'd said about tucking a five-dollar bill into the homeless guy's cup. Maybe he made it a habit to give money to others, which was unusual because, like cops, ADAs didn't make a lot of money. "Enjoy your sandwich."

She could tell that the moment his food was up, he planned to duck out of there. She tapped her foot, tugging on her boxy brown deputy uniform and the heavy bullet-resistant vest she wore beneath. The ugly color never bothered her before, but now she found herself wishing the handsome ADA could see her wearing something, anything else.

Even jeans and her favorite sweatshirt would be better than the tan shirt and brown slacks.

"Have a good day, Deputy Finnegan." ADA Scala scooped his sandwich bag off the counter and headed toward the door.

She wanted to call him back, ask him to wait for her, but sensed that would be akin to fighting a useless battle. Not that she was one to back down from a fight. Her gaze landed on the water bottle he'd inadvertently left behind. When her sandwich was ready, she grabbed her things and his water, then hurried after him.

"ADA Scala?" She shouted his title, hoping to catch him before he headed into the building. "You forgot your water!"

He spun to face her just as the sharp report of gunfire rang out.

"Down!" She dropped the items she'd been carrying, pulled her weapon from her hip holster, and sprinted toward him. "Get down!"

Another crack reverberated through the air as she threw herself over Scala's body, pinning him to the ground. Pedestrians on the street screamed and began to run in all different directions.

Grabbing her radio, she barked, "Shots fired outside the administrative building, Deputy Finnegan on scene and requesting backup!"

"What are you doing? Get off me." ADA Scala lifted himself up, dislodging her to the side.

"Stay down!" she yelled, climbing over his back, doing her best to cover him. "Can't you see I'm trying to protect you?" She swept her gaze over the location where the gunfire originated.

Whoever the perp was, he was gone now.

Made in the USA
Las Vegas, NV
28 June 2023